The Politician's Wife

'I've been an utter bloody fool, Flora.'

Flora braced herself. She knew now what those men were doing at the end of her drive, what Duncan was going to say. 'Who?'

'She's a researcher, or so I thought. It was a one-off, honestly. You must believe that.' Duncan's voice throbbed with sincerity; he almost believed it himself. He put his arms around her shoulders and shook her gently, as if to convince her. 'I was strung out. It was at the party conference.'

Shirley Lowe was women's editor of the *Sunday Mirror*, editor of *Over 21* magazine and a regular contributor to the *Express*, *The Times* and the *Independent*. She is the co-author of four novels, including the bestseller *Swapping*.

Shirley Lowe

The Politician's Wife

based on an original television series by Paula Milne,
produced for Channel Four Television by Producers Films

Mandarin
in association with Channel Four Television Corporation

A Mandarin Paperback
THE POLITICIAN'S WIFE

First published in Great Britain 1995
by Mandarin Paperbacks
an imprint of Reed Books Ltd
Michelin House, 81 Fulham Road, London SW3 6RB
and Auckland, Melbourne, Singapore and Toronto

Reprinted 1995

A CIP catalogue record for this title
is available from the British Library
ISBN 0 7493 2111 3

Typeset by Deltatype Ltd, Ellesmere Port, Cheshire
Printed and bound by Firmin-Didot (France),
Group Herissey. No d'impression : 31766.

I

The day before Flora Matlock's life fell apart she was sitting in a BBC television studio telling a group of teenagers about her wonderful husband and how lucky she was to be married to him.

Face the Famous, the programme on which Flora was a guest, is one of those late-afternoon programmes which encourages youth to fire questions at establishment figures in a frank, up-front manner, and to look self-consciously modish while they are doing it – nose rings on pretty girls, two-tone eye-shadow on butch boys, and cerise satin breeches on Donnie, the presenter. All of which made Flora, five foot six inches and conventionally pretty in a Home Counties Waitrose way, wish that she wasn't wearing her good grey dress and pearls.

'So what do you do?' a boy called out from the back of the group, in what Flora privately considered quite a rude manner. 'I mean, what sort of work does a politician's wife actually do?'

A series of images flashed through her mind. Knocking on inhospitable doors on cold, grey evenings instead of reading a bedtime story to Paul and Joanna. Standing under an umbrella at numerous fêtes and gymkhanas, handing out prizes and pinning on rosettes. Holding fragile, elderly hands, gazing into pale, anxious eyes – 'This is Norah, she's ninety-eight, aren't you, dear? We're all very proud of her.' Rallying the flagging faithful over endless cups of 'instant' in draughty halls. Turning up alone at speech days and sports days. 'Daddy sends his love, darling. You know how much he'd rather be here.'

And, Flora thought wryly, doing programmes like this.

'I help with all the constituency correspondence,' she said finally. 'That's a pretty full-time job in itself. And, of course, I go to all the constituency functions, formal receptions and so on. Since my husband became Minister for the Family he has so little time, you see . . . and Parliamentary politics can be pretty hectic . . .' (she briskly dismissed from her mind the steely in-fighting, the sharp knives in her husband's back) '. . . brutal, even. I try to keep him in touch with what's happening in the street, with the point of it all, if you like.'

Nice one, thought Donnie. Could have sounded pompous but it's come out dead sincere. 'You next, love.' He nodded at a girl almost concealed behind a cloud of auburn hair.

'What do you get out of it?' said the girl. 'For yourself, I mean.'

'Goodness . . . well . . .' Should she tell them, she wondered, how she'd felt that first time Duncan had won? Elated, triumphant. They'd fallen into each other's arms, laughing and crying, right there on the town hall podium as the Mayor read out the results. No, not laid back enough for these earnest young people. 'I suppose,' she said slowly and thoughtfully, 'if you're lucky enough to form a partnership with someone who has real value, a real ability to change things for the better, to enhance other people's lives, then it enhances your own life, just by being close to them.'

'Thank *you*, Mrs Matlock,' said Donnie. 'A real in-depth look there into the life of a Government Minister's better half.'

'You were brilliant, Mrs Matlock,' Phil, the director, said as they left the studio. 'A real pro. I'll get Allie, my PA, to send you a cassette of the programme, to show your husband. You've done him a bit of good today, I'd say.'

2

Flora smiled. She hoped it was true. It was, after all, why she was there.

'You'll be all right, then, will you? Can we get you a taxi?'

'No, no,' said Flora. 'My car's here. I've got to get back to Carlingham. The children will be coming home from school . . .'

'Good.' Phil shook Flora's hand briefly, his mind already in the cutting-room. He looked around distractedly for his PA, who was standing right behind him, clipboard in hand. 'Allie. Show Mrs Matlock down to the car-park, will you. And where's Donnie?'

'He's got to re-do the intro,' said Allie. 'He's in make-up.'

'Where else?' said Phil.

'She was really, really good, wasn't she?' Nerina, the make-up girl said, as she palmed gel onto Donnie's sleek black hair. 'Really natural.'

'Yeah. It was *Surprise! Surprise!* time when she started talking,' said Donnie. 'Nice-looking in a way, but that dreary grey serge, that dull hair and Jesus, that Alice-band. I thought it was going to be a hard slog all the way, but the lady certainly knows how to communicate. Did you see the body language when she was talking to the kids?'

'Sort of like Princess Di,' said Nerina. 'The way she got down amongst them when she was saying how she met him, you know, Duncan Thingy.'

'Matlock,' said Donnie.

'That's right. Duncan Matlock. When they met at Cambridge University at some debate about prisons . . .'

'Penal reform.'

'Same thing, isn't it?' Nerina slicked Donnie's hair with casual expertise. 'I wonder if she minds?'

'Minds what?'

'Well, I sort of got the impression she was, you know,

cleverer than him. I mean, they wouldn't have met at all if she hadn't gone up to him after the debate to put him right.'

'She did say he'd rather fudged a few facts,' Donnie agreed, 'but that's politicians for you.'

'I expect she fancied him rotten,' said Nerina. 'Can't think why. His hair's horrible.'

'It's charisma, Nerry, that's what it is.' Donnie gazed into the mirror admiringly. 'Charisma.'

Flora settled into the Volvo and buckled the safety belt. It had not been as alarming as she'd expected. How she dreaded these interviews, the personal questions. When she'd been asked what had attracted her to Duncan, she hadn't known what to say at first. Sexual chemistry, actually? The wilful curl behind his left ear? His unique ability to get taxis in the rain?

She couldn't explain to strangers how his idealism had touched her, his enthusiastic belief that he could take on the world for what he thought was right.

'His commitment?' she'd replied, eventually. 'His . . . basic morality, I suppose. It's quite a compelling combination.'

I know, Flora thought happily, as she pulled out at White City and headed towards the M40, I'll stop off at Marks & Sparks in Worcester on the way home and get some crumpets. We can toast them in front of the drawing-room fire when Paul and Joanna get back.

2

'Duncan Matlock's office.' Duncan's private secretary raised an urgent eyebrow at Mark Hollister, Special Adviser to the Minister for the Family, who was sifting papers at a large desk across the room from her. 'Sir Donald,' she mouthed. 'Wants to speak to the Minister.'

Mark picked up his phone. 'Mark Hollister, Sir Donald. Duncan's out and about, I'm afraid. Can I help?' There was a long pause before Mark put down the phone. He tapped it thoughtfully and said, his voice deliberately light, 'I'm going over to the House, Mary. Get Ian on the phone, tell him to call me as soon as possible. Preferably sooner.'

He took a piece of paper from a folder on his desk, stepped out of his Whitehall office and looked swiftly up and down the corridor. Thank God, nobody there. He glanced thoughtfully at the piece of paper in his hand, paused, folded it precisely into four and then sped off towards the lift.

'Afternoon, Mark.'

The stained-glass windows cast a hazy coloured light on the oak-panelled walls and, as Mark rounded a corner, he had failed to notice a colleague emerging from one of the many identical doors along the corridor. Instantly he modified his pace to a casual stroll, absurdly conscious of the piece of paper in his hand. 'Oh, hello James. Just going over to the House.'

'His Master's Voice?' said James. 'They can't manage without us, you know.'

'True, very true.' Mark nodded briefly. 'Must be off.'

'See you around, then,' said James. 'Will you be at the Policy Advisory meeting tomorrow?'

'Yes, yes. Well . . . probably.' Mark raised a hand. 'See you.' He quickened his pace and disappeared into the lift.

James looked after him. Odd fish, Hollister. Not like him to be so flustered. Must be up to something. Hard to tell what was going on behind those sinister rimless glasses, though.

This was probably the first time Mark had flashed his Commons pass and threaded his way through the bustling, tiled, central lobby without savouring the knowledge that he, Mark Hollister, the son of a Scunthorpe steel worker (long unemployed and long since deceased) had a rightful place in this historic setting. He darted up the stairs and into the Members' restaurant where the serious eaters were decimating the spotted dicks and jam roly-polys – no sign of his man. Along the corridor and into the Members' tea-room. There, groups of MPs were lunching lightly at the small tables. Some just gossiping together, others consulting their researchers or entertaining constituency visitors. A vista of grey suits with the occasional brave flash of colour from a female MP or guest. Sir Donald Frazier, chunky, reliable, the Tories' invaluable guru, sat in a far corner, wearing his customary, deceptively bohemian bow-tie, and talking earnestly to Ian Ruby-Smith, Duncan's Parliamentary Private Secretary. So Ian's in the picture then, Mark thought. Good. He walked over.

'Mark,' said Sir Donald, 'draw up a chair, grab a sandwich. We're going to need your advice.'

As Mark went over to the counter, Sir Donald turned back to Ian, speaking softly in what many MPs believed to be a skilfully preserved Scottish brogue. 'It's no-go with the *Mail*; usual tap-dance about public interest. He's going to have to front that one out. I'm still working on the others. I'll get on to the Chief Whip's office, we'll need a window later today. And tell Duncan to round up a war cabinet.' He straightened his shoulders. 'Read my lips, Ian, the forecast is for storms.'

An hour later Mark was on the phone to Colin Fletcher, Press and Information Officer at the Ministry for the Family. 'It's no comment, Colin. Have you got that? If anyone from the Press calls, verify nothing. Nothing, do you hear?'

Half an hour after that, he followed Duncan Matlock as he left his office – one of the coveted Ministerial sanctums conveniently situated right under the Chamber of the House – on his way to the Gents. As Duncan faced a urinal and unzipped, Mark moved into the vacant stall next to him, took the folded piece of paper out of his pocket and passed it to his Minister. Duncan glanced at the piece of paper. His face muscles tightened momentarily but he managed a wary smile.

Strolling over to the basin he passed a stolid back-bencher from the Shires, and, composure regained, greeted him: 'Another Select Committee, John? You'll need a season ticket at this rate.'

'PR tour with some bloody blue-rinse constituents,' said the back-bencher. 'All I bloody need.'

Duncan laughed easily and gave the Member from the Shires a playful punch on the shoulder. He turned on the taps and saw, reflected behind him in the mirror, Mark Hollister's pale, sombre face. Their eyes met. 'Relax, my friend,' Duncan said softly, 'this is not the end. Believe me, it is not even the beginning of the end.'

He grinned at Mark, whose pale, liquid eyes, masked behind his glasses, glinted back at him. The cool bastard, Mark thought. Maybe, just maybe, he'll pull this one off.

In Duncan's office the war cabinet was in action. Amid a cacophony of barked commands and ringing phones a secretary, taking a call, was wheedling, 'But he has to get in to see the Chief Whip today. Can't you slide him in between appointments? Oh, *thank* you.'

Ian Ruby-Smith, Duncan's PPS, was hunched over a phone, also wheedling. 'The story breaks tomorrow, we can't wait that long. Can't you re-route me on to his mobile?' Clapping a hand over the mouthpiece, he called over to Colin Fletcher. 'How about your pal at ITN? Is he solid?'

Colin, who was explaining to an *Express* reporter for the fifth time that his Minister was not available for comment, stopped only briefly to reflect that when he took this job he had visualised himself discussing meaningful matters of State over a civilised lunch in the Carlton; not calling in all his contacts to avert a squalid personal scandal. However, this was undoubtedly his part of ship and he'd better act willing. 'I'll get on to him. And how about seeing if we've got a tame Governor at the Beeb?'

'Good idea.' And not before bloody time, Ian muttered to himself. Wasn't a Press and Information Officer meant to be adept at informing the Press? 'We could try Baroness Bryson, every Board's token female; she's on the Board of Governors at the Beeb and gentle words of womanly wisdom might be particularly appropriate in this case. Sir Donald is an old chum of hers; perhaps he can do à bit of lobbying in that direction.'

Glancing across the room, Ian observed Mark Hollister, tight-lipped, his body tensed with a strange, inner excitement, hissing commands down his phone. 'No, no, he's not a player. We need a heavyweight who can steer this thing from the off. Do a round-robin of all the back-benchers you can reach. Someone on the Exec of the 1992 might be handy. Ditto the twenty-two, and if you get a chance, poke your nose into the Reform . . .'

In the inner office, Duncan Matlock paced up and down

with his mobile phone. 'A chum at Fortress Wapping alerted us a week ago,' he said. 'We tried for an injunction but it slipped through the net.' Slamming down the aerial on his mobile, he shouted over to his secretary. 'Get Mark to call my father-in-law and Roger Gravely, my solicitor, will you? Say it's a red alert to get over to my home double-quick.'

Ian, who had the uneasy feeling that he was not going to get back to *his* home in Weybridge in time for the pleasant game of bridge he and his wife had planned, was suddenly aware that the whole room seemed to be quite enjoying itself. Eyes were glittering, as though the Ministry for the Family had suddenly discovered some particularly satisfactory drink or drug. Which, of course, Ian realised, it had. As anyone who has ever sailed close to the wind knows, nothing in the world gives you a better high than a dangerous roll of adrenalin.

3

Flora pulled into the drive and surveyed her *acers* with approval. When she and Duncan had found Mindermere House they had been charmed instantly by the ivy-covered red brick and then by the the sprawling spaciousness of the high-ceilinged rooms. Even during the first walk-around with the estate agent, Flora could envisage the warmth of faded Oriental rugs on the flagged hall-floor, the comfort of an Aga in the big family kitchen (with walk-in larder, she'd always craved that), a roaring fire casting shadows in the pine-panelled drawing-room. But it was the *acers* in the shrubbery that had swung it for her.

They could afford it – just – if Flora was prepared to sacrifice most of the salary Duncan paid her for constituency and secretarial work. It seemed she was. 'Angel,' Duncan had said, kissing her. 'Nobody else would tackle thousands of boring letters *and* Mrs Rosalind Clegg, in exchange for some rather weedy trees.'

He approved the house because it was bang in the middle of his constituency ('You can nurse the worthies while I'm in London, sweetheart') yet close to the motorway. ('I'll find a little *pied-à-terre* in town and whizz down at weekends.')

Flora's old schoolfriend, Charlotte, had advised against the plan. 'It's madness, Flora, and you know it. What's he going to be up to in London while you're embalmed in the provinces? He'll soon tire of the solitary baked bean. All those leggy secretaries and researchers in the House, you've read about them, for God's sake.'

'But I'll be going up to town most weeks,' Flora had said. 'Duncan says it'll be super for the theatre – and we can keep up with our London friends.'

In fact, she very rarely got to London. There was so much to do in the constituency, besides all that correspondence. Rosalind Clegg, the vice-chairman of the local Conservative Association had signed her up for charity committees, fête appearances and fund-raising events before she'd even laid the stair carpets. And Veronica Weston of the Conservative Christian Wives' Association was equally keen for her to help out with the WI, the Single Mothers' Hostel and such pressing church matters as the appeal for a new organ and a regular, tasteful display of flowers for the altar. As wife of the Minister for the Family, Flora felt she could hardly refuse. And then there was the immutable school run, which was a different matter altogether.

Flora enjoyed standing outside St Mary's (she hoped Mrs Weston didn't know that it was a *Roman Catholic* school) with the other mothers, watching the little girls spill joyously out into the small front courtyard. And when she'd collected Joanna (usually last because she'd been told to go back and tie her shoe-laces), and her noisy clutch of friends, she'd drive on to pick up Paul and his more sedate set of eleven-year-olds from Carlingham College.

There was a smell of damp hair in the car that Wednesday afternoon, because Joanna's class had been swimming. Dashing into the house, she dropped her wet towel and swim-suit on the oak chest in the hall and, accompanied by Basker the labrador, rapturously pleased to welcome them home, made for the playroom.

Flora picked up the bathing things. 'Joanna. Take these to Mrs Lucas and then go upstairs and wash that chlorine out of your hair.'

'But what about *Neighbours*?' Joanna turned on the television. 'The baby's been kidnapped.'

'I don't care if it's been barbecued,' Flora said. 'Just do it. Please? And Paul. Go upstairs and start your homework, darling. I'll be up in a minute.'

And why, Flora wondered guiltily, does my voice always sound so much more tender when I'm talking to Paul? True, he was her first-born, two years older than Joanna, but that wasn't why he tugged at her heart-strings. It was, she realised, the metal specs that kept slipping off his nose, the gasping attacks of asthma he tried to conceal because he knew how much it worried her. He always seemed to her so dangerously vulnerable.

Joanna came whirling out of the playroom and raced up the stairs. 'If I go and wash my hair now,' she said, 'can I stay up for *Brookside*?'

'No, oh, I suppose so.' Flora was thinking how little time it took for Joanna to accept an ultimatum and go into renegotiation mode and how very like her father this was, when Mrs Lucas, the housekeeper, came into the hall.

'I'll deal with those, Mrs Matlock.' She took the bathing things from Flora. 'Oh, and your husband's office just rang. It seems the Press are pestering him about something. They said not to answer the phone, to put all the answer things on, and Mr Matlock will be home later to see to them himself.'

'Duncan? Coming home?' said Flora. 'But it's only Wednesday.'

'Around ten or so, they thought.'

'In that case, Mrs Lucas,' said Flora, 'you'd better de-frost the game pie and see how we are on the Haagen Dazs front.'

'Leave it to me.' Mrs Lucas strode briskly into the kitchen and Flora crouched on the floor, hugging Basker. 'Daddy coming home to see us mid-week, Baskers? Aren't we lucky?'

12

*

The meeting with the Chief Whip had been an anti-climax. Did I expect him, Duncan wondered, to wave a wand and magic away the last few hours? The truth was, he'd expected exactly that, and back on his office, running the gamut of questioning eyes, it was an effort to look confident and relaxed.

Mark followed him into the inner office and closed the door. 'How did it go?'

'It seems the PM is *en route* from Strasbourg, so we've got a bit of time to get our ducks in a row,' Duncan said.

'Quite,' said Mark, 'but is he cranking up the party machine and giving us maximum back-up?'

'Not exactly,' Duncan said cautiously. What the Chief Whip had actually said was that he had no wish to sit in judgement on his fellow Members but, at a time when the party was talking Family Values, this kind of thing was not doing them any favours. Particularly, he'd added, when it involved the Minister for the Family. But, as Duncan had assured him that this was a one-off error which would not be repeated, he would, of course, do everything within his power to help; and he had briskly brought the meeting to an end by saying that he knew Duncan would excuse him if he turfed him out, because he had a three-line whip to organise for the morrow. 'He said he'd do what he could to help.'

'Hmm.' Mark looked bleakly out of the window at the groups of reporters and cameramen gathered in the street below. 'Are you prepared to face the pack, then?'

The afternoon's adrenalin had seeped away by the time Duncan, briefcase in hand, flanked by Mark and Ian Ruby-Smith, stepped tentatively out of his office on to the steps of Number 1 Whitehall. Moving towards the car, he was immediately surrounded by reporters and photographers, surging and shouting.

'Any comment on tomorrow's story, Mr Matlock?'

'Look this way, Mr Matlock!'

'Is it true your injunction to quash the story failed, Minister?'

'The story is you were together as recently as last month. Can you confirm that, Mr Matlock?'

Duncan squared his shoulders, forced a smile. Mustn't let the bastards see they were getting to him. 'No comment.'

Between them, Mark and Ian hustled Duncan into the car, but the reporters were running, avid faces pressed against the window.

'What does your wife have to say about it, Minister?'

'Does this mean you'll be stepping down as Minister for the Family, Mr Matlock?'

Duncan mustered a look of concern mingled with a wry smile of contempt for the mêlée as the car pulled out into the rush-hour traffic. By the time they got to the motorway he was slumped in a corner, his eyes closed, trying to shut out the nightmare scenario unfolding before him.

Mark was on the car phone. Duncan wished he couldn't hear any of it: '. . . failing the MD, anyone on the Board you can access. And *The Times* is still a loose cannon. Good man, thanks.' He hung up. 'Duncan?'

'Okay, recap.' Duncan's eyes were still closed.

'Two fronts need shoring up. Priority one, the local Conservative Association.'

'Which could go either way.'

'Exactly. And then the back-benchers. The 1922 is the key one there.'

'The Chief Whip will do the trench work on that.'

'If history is any precedent, they'll take their cue from each other,' said Mark.

'How does that thing go?' Duncan gazed out sightlessly at the passing countryside. 'The dog, to suit some private ends, went mad and bit the man. The man recovered from the bite, it was the dog that died. Jesus, Mark, if Margaret was still holding the reins we'd have this thing airtight by now.'

Mark made a note in his diary. 'I'll reschedule that dinner you cancelled.'

Duncan rounded on him. 'No, no, use your head, man,' he said sharply. 'See how the dice roll first. To beat the establishment you need its prime movers at your side, not some maverick sideshow.'

Mark would have liked to respond that Duncan was in no position to speak to his Special Adviser in that bloody arrogant manner, but he didn't bother. He had a more effective weapon than words in his briefcase. He took out a newspaper cutting and handed it to Duncan. 'I dug this up,' he said.

'What?'

'The *Mail on Sunday* ran a feature on Tory wives last autumn.'

It was full-page colour picture of Flora. Duncan gazed at the photograph and Flora gazed back at him – trusting, guileless and with that familiar, quirky half-smile he had always found infinitely appealing. He traced the shape of her face gently with his finger; his wife, his lover, his best friend. Oh God, what a bloody mess.

'You've seen the headline, of course?' said Mark, who was not getting the reaction he'd hoped.

'Headline?' Duncan looked down at the cutting again and read, in double-bold caps, 'IF MY HUSBAND WAS UNFAITH-FUL I'D LEAVE, says Mrs Duncan Matlock.'

Duncan shook himself back to reality, grinned at Mark and handed back the cutting. 'You mustn't believe everything you read in the newspapers, Mark.'

Flora and Paul were cosily settled in Paul's room, tackling a maths textbook. Basker was curled up on the rug, grunting companionably in his sleep.

'The decimal point should be here, for a start,' said Flora. 'That's your problem.'

'There goes the telephone again,' Paul said. 'Shouldn't we answer it?'

'Daddy says no,' said Flora, 'it's business. Oh, for heaven's sake, there it is again.' It had often occurred to her that whoever coined the irritating phrase 'quality time' had been trying to describe the quiet half-hour she often spent with Paul in his room, monitoring his homework. And now it was being ruined by some wretched Westminster drama; she only hoped Duncan hadn't made some impulsive statement in the House again. 'Question six, Paul,' she said in a motivating sort of voice, 'you haven't even started it.'

But Paul wasn't listening. He was staring abstractedly out of the window. 'Who are those people?'

Flora followed his glance. At the end of the drive a small group of people were gathering. And one or two of them, she noted, were carrying cameras.

'Press, darling. Daddy has some sort of kerfuffle on. Ignore them. Now, question six. Aloud, please.'

Paul read aloud (the only bit of maths homework he didn't mind doing): 'If a train is travelling at 170 miles per hour over a distance of 90 miles, how long does it take to reach its destination?' He looked hopefully at his mother but she wasn't listening. Now she was gazing out of the window.

'Sorry, pet,' she said. 'But I'm sure that's grandad's Rover down there . . . and Daddy's solicitor, Mr Gravely and . . .' Yes, definitely, unmistakably Hugo Patterson, the constituency party chairman, looking, even from Flora's bird's-eye view, dauntingly formidable. She put an arm around Paul's shoulders. 'You carry on, darling. I'd better go down and see what on earth is going on.'

Carrying the drinks tray, Flora paused at the study door. She could hear her father's voice, holding forth knowledgeably, a murmur of assent.

She tapped at the door. 'Daddy?'

Her father opened the door. Clive Woodley, a one-time property developer who had invested his money wisely, at the right time, and who looked as though he had enjoyed many a convivial business lunch along the way, reached out to take the tray.

'I couldn't find the tonic or soda, so I thought sherry?' Still holding the tray, Flora attempted to see beyond her father's bulky figure into the study.

'Just what the doctor ordered.' Clive stood firm and hoped to God Duncan would get back soon and that he wouldn't have to break the ghastly news to his only child. 'Bless you, Flo. We can manage from here.' He took the tray from Flora and retreated into the study, closing the door behind him.

Flora was left in the hall, listening again to the urgent murmurings on the other side of the door. She was wondering whether to have a surreptitious listen or to bang on the door and say, 'Hold on a minute, this is my house. What on earth's going on?' when there was a knock at the front door.

She turned to open it, but Mrs Lucas beat her to it. The man standing on the doorstep had the dodgy look of a professional charmer. 'Just a quick word with Mrs Matlock, love, then I'm history,' he said.

'How many times do I have to tell you all?' said Mrs Lucas, who didn't care to be called 'love' by anyone except Mr Lucas. 'Please go and wait at the bottom of the drive with the others.' She started closing the door.

'Hold it.' The reporter had spotted Flora. 'That's her . . . Mrs Matlock, Mrs Matlock. Any comment on tomorrow's story in . . .'

Mrs Lucas slammed the door shut. 'I'll just see to the supper, then,' she said and, avoiding the question in Flora's eyes, moved swiftly towards the kitchen.

A tight knot of anxiety was twisting in Flora's stomach. A sort of indigestion pain, only worse. She diagnosed it, disconcertingly, as foreboding. Slowly, she followed Mrs Lucas into the kitchen and, for a moment, stood in the doorway, enjoying the familiar surroundings. The red kettle boiling cheerily on the black Aga, the cupboards she'd had made specially out of old pine doors, the wild flowers Joanna had collected on a field study course standing in a jam jar on the pine table. Mrs Lucas, hard-working, loyal, a reliable back-up whenever Flora had to go to London or got stuck in a meeting, was preparing a supper tray for the children; doing ordinary things like washing lettuce, cutting up tomatoes, breaking hard-boiled eggs. And, as usual, the radio was going full blast. Flora smiled affectionately. Mrs Lucas couldn't work without a constant input from Radio 4. She was just going over to the fridge to take out the ham when she – and Flora – became aware of what the newsreader was saying.

'. . . sensational revelations in tomorrow's newspapers regarding Duncan Matlock, Minister for the Family. Mr Matlock was unavailable for comment . . .'

Mrs Lucas quickly switched off the radio and turned to see Flora standing in the doorway. 'Oh.' She cleared her throat nervously. 'I thought I'd eat in the playroom with the children, if that's all right?'

'Fine,' said Flora. 'Whatever.'

Mrs Lucas picked up the tray. Still avoiding Flora's eyes, she stopped *en route* to the door. 'I can stay over if it would help? Help you with the children or . . . ?'

'That's won't be necessary.' And then, touched by the

older woman's obvious unease, Flora put a hand on Mrs Lucas's arm. 'But thank you, anyway.'

She waited until she heard Mrs Lucas opening the playroom door, and then went swiftly to the radio and turned it on again.

'. . . just when the UN troops are trapped in the crossfire between . . .'

There was a splinter of determination in Flora's face as she turned off the radio, walked purposefully over to the study door and opened it. 'Daddy,' she said. 'Do you have a minute?'

4

'Duncan's in trouble, isn't he?' Flora stood in the dining-room and gazed out through the casement windows at the strange goings-on at the bottom of her drive. A gaggle of reporters by the gate, another group of reporters huddled inside a parked car, even more reporters silhouetted in the headlights of another parked car.

'Yes.' Clive positioned himself on the other side of the polished refectory table. He'd never found it easy to talk to his daughter. Not about the things that mattered, anyway. Ever since Marjorie died . . . Well, a girl needed her mother. He took a deep breath. 'We're counting on you to be a team player in this, Flo.'

Flora stared at her father, perplexed. 'What on earth do you mean, Daddy?'

'I only know the barest of details, my dear.'

Flora determinedly met his eyes. 'I want to know, Daddy.'

Clive looked away, trapped. He took a deep breath, and then exhaled with relief as a car pulled up outside and Duncan stepped out of it. 'I'll let him tell you himself, my dear.' He went over to Flora and kissed her tentatively on the forehead. 'Be strong, Flora.'

Flora couldn't remember the last time her father had kissed her. On her graduation day? At her wedding? It only increased her anxiety.

Gratefully, Clive rose to greet Duncan, arms outstretched. 'Duncan.' They embraced awkwardly.

'Clive, thanks for coming over,' said Duncan, 'Is Roger here?'

'In the study.' Clive was relieved to be dealing with facts rather than emotions. 'Patterson, too.'

Before Flora was able to say anything, Mark Hollister had come into the room. 'Flora . . .' She noticed that he, too, had trouble meeting her eyes.

'Mark . . . ?'

There was a tap on the window . . . faces, the flash of cameras. Swiftly, Duncan drew the curtains. 'Clive, take Mark on through, will you. I'll join you in a minute. And turn the answering machines off. The PM's due to call.'

The two men left the room gratefully and Duncan turned slowly to face Flora. 'Damned prying eyes. Have they been bothering you much?'

'What's happening, Duncan?' Flora looked directly at her husband.

Duncan didn't answer. Instead, he strode across the room, took one of her hands and kissed it. The gesture was tender and unexpected and, before Flora could respond, Duncan had taken her by the hand and led her through the kitchen, out the back door, across the lawn and into the Orangery.

'It's raining.' Flora pushed her hand through her hair. She could feel the raindrops, hear them hitting the glass roof and walls.

Duncan, still in his overcoat, switched on the light. The fragrant scent of Flora's lovingly nurtured philadelphus filled the air. She watched Duncan touch the white buds, bend to catch their scent.

With his face still buried in the blossom, he said: 'Remember when we last sheltered in here from the rain at Joanna's birthday party? There was that tedious little man we rented the bouncy castle from and he came in here after us. We couldn't get shot of him.'

Flora wasn't remembering the bouncy man. She was remembering the day Joanna was born. Duncan at her side, delightedly cradling the tiny baby, not minding the blood and the mess, crying out: 'It's a girl, my clever one,' and kissing her. 'A boy and a girl. Now we're a proper family.'

'I've been an utter bloody fool, Flora.'

Flora braced herself. She knew now what those men were doing at the end of her drive, what Duncan was going to say. 'Who?'

'She's a researcher, or so I thought. It was a one-off, honestly. You must believe that.' Duncan's voice throbbed with sincerity; he almost believed it himself. He put his arm around her shoulders and shook her gently, as if to convince her. 'I was strung out. It was at the party conference.'

'I was at the party conference,' Flora said.

'You left early, to check out that tutor for Paul, remember?' Duncan was speaking rapidly now. His subconscious was sending him a message – this is the first hurdle, then Patterson, the PM – 'She was at the reception on the last day. There had been all that aggro over my speech. Then that amazing ovation. I was on a roll, sweetheart. I got back to London. You weren't there and she called me, it was totally unexpected. I'm not making excuses. There is no excuse, I know that.' He pulled Flora roughly to him, buried his face in her neck. 'It was your face I saw, my darling. All the time. Only yours. I swear it.'

Flora was limp in his arms. There was a terrible blankness in her eyes. Duncan winced. He could feel her pain as if it were his own.

'God, Flora,' he murmured, 'hate the sin, yes. Of course. But not the sinner. Please don't hate me.'

Flora wrenched herself out of Duncan's arms. She had to get away, be alone. She couldn't listen to any more. As she ran out into the rain, she heard him call after her: 'Flora, come back! Flora!' She clapped her hands over her ears. At an upstairs window, Paul, still wrestling with the problem of the 170 mph train, saw the stricken figure of his mother stumbling through the rain, up the lawn, towards the house.

Duncan shivered slightly. It's the overcoat, he told himself, it's wet. He shrugged himself out of the navy blue Melton and hung it up in the back porch with the wellies and Barbours, where it looked oddly out of place.

It had been worse than he'd expected, much worse. He rubbed his hands together to keep warm: he was still shivering – the tension of the day was getting to him. Going to the fridge, he took out a tub of Haagen Dazs and studied the label. Cookies 'n' Cream, that's the one. Nursery food, comfort food. He sat down, swung his feet up on the pine table, and eagerly spooned up the ice-cream, straight from the tub.

It hadn't been true, of course, that bit about seeing Flora's face – she'd been the very last thing on his mind at the time. But, funny thing, sitting here, his eyes closed, he could see her face all too clearly. That look of blank, numbed hurt. He wondered if she would always be there, reproaching him, every time he closed his eyes.

'Duncan?' Clive entered the kitchen, diffidently.

Duncan was suddenly overwhelmed by a rush of gratitude. It was his father-in-law who had financed his first faltering political steps, and introduced him to the constituency party chairman Hugo Patterson, an old business associate. ('I've done Hugo one or two favours in the past, Duncan,' Clive had said. 'I think you'll find him sympathetic.') There couldn't be many men who would rush to the aid of the man who had messed up their daughter's life, could there? Duncan felt a chill of regret. And, quite possibly, their grandchildren's lives, too? Pushing aside the tub of ice-cream along with the uncomfortable thought, he reached out a hand to Clive: 'You've been a fucking marvel over this, Clive. You really have.'

Clive gave Duncan's hand a brief grip of affectionate, masculine solidarity. 'You're my son, Duncan, in all but name. And what the hell's in a name, anyway?' He looked up at the ceiling apprehensively. 'Do you think I should go up?'

'No, give her a minute.' Duncan pulled out a chair.

'It's a bad business.' Clive sat down gratefully, and realised, with a *frisson* of guilt, that he was not thinking so much of his daughter, quite probably sobbing her heart out upstairs, but of himself. All his hopes and ambitions were invested in Duncan. 'Anything I can do?'

'God, I'm bloody bushwhacked already, and this is only round one.' Duncan leaned back in his chair, stretching to relieve the fatigue creeping over him. 'Best thing you can do at this moment in time, Clive, is to keep on sweet-talking Patterson. How's he taking it so far?'

'He's rattled,' said Clive. 'He reckons there's a few in the Association who could make waves.'

'You know Heseltine's cardinal rule? Avoid confrontation unless you can choose the moment for it.' Duncan paused, and then said, very slowly: 'If the Press get even a whiff of my Bill it won't be Ministry of the Family so much as Ministry of Famine.'

'But won't Sir Donald handle the Press?' Clive asked anxiously. 'Isn't that why the PM's got him on the case?'

'Yes, but he'll be operating more of a covert operation, won't he? What we need now is a public statement of support from Downing Street, and if Flora doesn't stick . . .'

'She will,' Clive said with certainty. He was already on his feet.

Flora was curled up on her bed in a foetal position,

protecting herself, the way she'd done that first term at boarding-school. She wasn't crying any more, there were no tears left. She was staring, fixedly, at the dressing-table. Those silver brushes, that comb with one tooth missing, the photograph in a pretty antique frame showing herself, Duncan, and the children, carefree and laughing during a Sunday walk on the Clents, with Basker racing after a stick. The shopping list she'd made only that morning – it seemed a lifetime away. Everything in its proper place, just the same as usual, only nothing was the same any more.

There was a knock at the door, but Flora didn't move. 'Mum?'

'Coming, darling.' Quickly, Flora jumped up from the bed, smoothed her skirt, rubbed the tearstains from her cheeks and opened the door. Paul was standing on the landing in his pyjamas, holding his asthma inhaler. He was deathly pale and his breathing was harsh, unnaturally fast.

Flora took the inhaler, crouched down beside Paul and put it gently into his mouth. 'In and out,' she said, 'you know how. That's the way.'

Gradually, Paul's breathing relaxed and Flora removed the inhaler. Paul studied his mother's face gravely and then reached out to touch the tearstains. 'Did he do that?'

Somewhere in the back of her mind, Flora recognised the rejection implicit in 'he' rather than 'Daddy.' It would have been so easy and so unfair to share her pain with Paul, and she was relieved to hear herself saying, quite firmly, 'No, I did.' She rallied a smile. 'Now, you run along to the playroom and choose a video. I'll come and watch it with you soon.'

'Promise?'

'Promise.'

Paul put his arms around her. 'You're the best,' he said.

'And you're the second best,' said Flora, following their familiar ritual.

She watched Paul go slowly downstairs, and then went back into her room and, drained of emotion, leaned against the closed door. Almost immediately there was another knock.

Clive came in and switched on the light.

'No!' said Flora. He mustn't see her anguish.

Switching off the light, Clive stood there in the gloom, large and awkward, as if uncertain where to begin. Eventually, he sat on the bed and patted a place beside him. Flora remained, gazing blankly ahead, as though she was asleep standing up, and this was just a nightmare. Soon she would wake up . . .

Clive started speaking slowly, testing the ground. 'When your mother died in that car, you know what got me through, Flo? I thought of it as a test . . . it had been waiting for me all along . . . that my life had been a preparation for that one moment . . .' he looked hopefully at Flora '. . . the moment when I decided not to go under. But to survive.'

Flora's expression didn't change. 'When did he tell you?'

'We hoped to protect you, darling.'

'When?'

Clive ignored the question and continued with his carefully prepared script. 'You could have gone for a banker, my dear, or a dentist. You didn't. You chose the fast track. You chose Duncan. There's always a price tag.' He waited for some sign that he was making contact. There was none. 'She flattered him. You know how these things go. How weak we men are.'

There was a flash of something in Flora's eyes. Revulsion? Anger? Contempt? Clive quickly tried another tack. 'You're the rock upon which his whole life rests, Flora. Political, personal, the whole kit and caboodle. I know you're suffering, darling. He is, too. And he's going to suffer a lot more before this thing is over, believe you me. He needs you now, more than ever.'

Flora looked wearily at her father. She had always known it, never wanted to admit it. This was not a shoulder to cry on, nor a man to rely on. 'Go downstairs, Daddy, please.'

'What do you say I call a chum?' Clive said desperately. 'Charlotte, perhaps? Get her to come over?'

'No,' said Flora sharply.

'Surely, darling, there's somebody who . . . ?'

'You're wrong, Daddy,' Flora interrupted him harshly. 'I didn't choose Duncan, he chose me.' She could see them now, all wondering why Duncan Matlock, President of the Union, rugby blue, the man every girl yearned to dance and flirt with at the May Ball, had chosen dull, quiet Flora Woodley. Sitting over a coffee in the Whim, strolling hand in hand around Parker's Piece, whenever they were together . . . she could see the question in everyone's eyes. 'I don't want them here,' she said bleakly. 'Any of them.'

Sir Donald Frazier's journey from London had been bloody awful. Accident on the motorway, flashing lights, a two-mile tailback, cones all over the place. And ahead he could see another obstruction. Cars, reporters, cameramen, sprawled all over the roads leading to Mindermere House.

'Take the next left, Jenkins,' he said to his chauffeur. 'We'll approach from the rear, as it were.'

'Right you are, sir.' Jenkins wheeled the Jaguar round in a satisfying screech, the way they do on the telly, and shot off down a dirt track. 'Can't go any further, sir,' he said. 'Dead-end.'

'Right.' Sir Donald jumped out of the car. 'I'll leg it from here. Stick around, Jenkins.'

He pushed his way through a gap in a hedge, and, rather

wishing that the PM or his staid children could see him, he circumnavigated a vegetable garden, and made for the light of the house. Once inside, tie awry, shoes muddied, he pulled off his mac, hung it in the porch and charged into the kitchen, just as Clive Woodley came in from the hall.

'Sir Donald. Thank God,' said Clive. 'It's been like waiting for the cavalry to arrive.'

'Where is he?' Sir Donald looked around, as though he expected Duncan to spring out of a broom cupboard.

'In the study,' said Clive. 'Talking to the PM.'

'Well, lead the way,' said Sir Donald.

The atmosphere in the study was cosy but tense: a roaring fire, and decanters of whisky and sherry gleaming invitingly on the table. Roger Gravely, the family solicitor, was sitting in a wing chair. Across the fireplace sat Hugo Patterson, the constituency party chairman, dealing with a large cigar, blowing smoke rings. Mark Hollister was standing with his back to the fire. They were all tensely absorbed in Duncan's telephone conversation.

'I can't tell you how wretched I feel about this, Prime Minister . . .' – he raised an eyebrow in greeting to Sir Donald – 'Sir Donald's just arrived. I will . . . yes . . .' He mouthed a greeting from the PM to Sir Donald, who poured himself a large whisky and went over to warm himself by the fire. 'Naturally, if there's the slightest chance this might jeopardise the party, or your own standing, my resignation will be on your desk by the morning . . .' Sir Donald and Mark exchanged a look, bracing themselves for the PM's response. 'She's rock-solid,' Duncan was saying, 'absolutely behind me one hundred per cent. I'll tell her . . . thank you. I appreciate that. We both do.' Duncan hung up and looked around at the men assembled in his study. 'He doesn't see it as a resigning issue.'

'Thank God,' said Roger.

'Recent history suggests that, nevertheless, we should not be too sanguine,' Sir Donald said.

'Quite,' said Duncan. 'He did add a caveat. "At the moment." He said it was up to me to ride the beast.'

Clive, who had been looking from one to the other, searching for a guiding clue, said: 'In other words, he'll hold the course if we do?'

'Exactly.' Hugo Patterson nodded. 'The important thing is that we're still in the ring.'

As Sir Donald rolled up his sleeves and opened his briefcase the atmosphere in the room lightened, as though it were a signal that the waiting was over and the action about to begin. 'The secret, gentlemen,' said Donald, looking around the room like a conjurer preparing to stun his audience with a particularly showy trick, 'is not to minimise the impact of what has occurred but to subvert it to our own advantage. Presentation is all.'

'Ah,' Clive nodded. He knew about presentation. 'That speech you're due to give at the Family Policy Forum, Duncan. We'll need to focus on that.'

'Is this really an opportune moment for Duncan to address the FPF?' said Mark Hollister. 'I can see the headlines now, and they're using words like "hypocrite" and "brazen". Even' – there was the hint of a superior smile which Sir Donald found deeply irritating – ' "ill-judged"?'

'Couldn't be a more opportune moment if it's handled correctly,' Sir Donald said briskly. 'I spent a useful couple of hours in the Garrick before I left town. And, after putting out a few feelers and a few judiciously applied brandies, managed to persuade Barton, Benson, Hennessey & Phipps to draft Jeremy Phipps over to Smith Square for the next few weeks.'

'An advertising man?' said Roger, who didn't hold with

29

advertising men – particularly the noisy group that invariably blocked him at the fourteenth hole every Sunday morning.

'The best communicator in the country,' said Sir Donald. 'He'll write your speech for you, Duncan.' Duncan started to demur, and Sir Donald added quickly, 'While taking account of your valuable input, of course. And it will then be down to you to deliver the talk with proper humility and sincerity. All right, so far?' He didn't expect or wait for an answer. 'Now, this is a schedule for the next twenty-four hours. Starting, Duncan, with a photo-call at nine tomorrow morning for you, Flora and the children. Oh, and Jeremy thought it would be a nice touch if you were there, Clive, a sort of family endorsement.'

'Count on me,' said Clive.

'We'll hold Duncan's folks as back-up. Then you'll have to face the firing squad at the local Association, Duncan. And that's where you come in, Patterson.'

'I've already got out a call to arms,' said Hugo Patterson. 'It's a close-run thing at the moment, but it's my bet that if Flora is solid, they will be.'

'Right,' said Sir Donald. 'And how is Flora?'

Duncan looked swiftly at Clive, who gave an almost imperceptible shrug and said: 'Still rather reeling, I'm afraid.'

'Dear God, man.' Sir Donald turned to Duncan in disbelief. 'Then what on earth are you doing down here?'

Flora was not in the bedroom, but there were two open suitcases on the bed strewn with her clothes: cupboards were agape and open drawers spewed out their contents, as though a particularly assiduous burglar had been at work. Duncan groaned and, dashing along the landing, pulled up short outside Joanna's room. She was sitting on her bed, sleepily tugging on her socks. Flora was at the chest of drawers, stuffing a suitcase with clothes.

'Flora?' Duncan said tentatively.

Flora looked straight through him and continued packing. 'You'll need shoes, darling, your blue ones,' she was saying, 'and your anorak.'

As Flora picked up the case and walked swiftly past Duncan and out of the room, he sensed a dangerous tautness about her, like a coiled spring.

'We're going on holiday, Daddy,' Joanna said. 'Did Mummy tell you?'

Duncan didn't hear her. He was intent on getting back to the bedroom before Flora went downstairs with her suitcases and ruined everything. He raced past Paul's bedroom, only vaguely registering that his son, too, was stuffing a rucksack with clothes.

'Flora?'

She was moving around their room, opening and closing drawers, collecting up more clothes, pushing them haphazardly into the cases. Her actions were mechanical, as though she were moving in a dream.

'I'm taking the children away for a few days,' she said. 'I need to think.' She didn't trust herself to look at Duncan.

'Don't do this, Flora.' Duncan followed her around the room. 'Hear me out. Please. She head-hunted me, honestly. She and her boyfriend set a trap and I was mug enough to walk into it.'

'Did you walk, Duncan, or did you run?' Flora yanked the hairdryer plug out of the socket, fumbling as she wound the flex round the machine. Her voice was flat and dreary as she said: 'I've seen you look at women. Often. In the street . . . at parties. I've always told myself, so long as he looks, he won't touch.'

'And I haven't,' said Duncan. 'Not before this. Not once.'

He could hear his voice rising and, conscious of the men waiting downstairs in his study, deliberately dropped a decibel. 'Think of everything we've worked for, Flora. Everything we've achieved, we've done together. Look around you. At the house. Our home. Our children. Right from the beginning we've been a team.'

Flora snapped a case shut, and it seemed to Duncan as though his last slither of hope was being closed inside it. 'Remember,' he said, 'when we sat through that bloody selection interview? You were the one with all the answers, Flora. I relied on you for that. I always have.'

Yes, Flora thought, as she folded a silk blouse and shoved it in another case, I remember the selection committe. Being cross-questioned and interviewed for somebody else's job. And being stupid enough to feel a stab of pride when I overheard a piggy man say to a patronising woman, 'Nice sensible girl, just the sort of wife we need for the constituency.'

'They looked at you, at your decency and your honesty, and I gained respect for that,' said Duncan – he might almost have been reading her thoughts – 'They admired me for having the wit to choose a woman like you for my wife. Okay, I lost my bearings for a while . . .' Suddenly, exasperated by Flora's interminable packing and lack of response, he snatched the clothes from her hands: 'For God's sake, stop that!'

Flora, motionless, said simply: 'What's her name?'

'What?' Duncan, clutching a pale-blue cashmere sweater and a pair of tights, was nonplussed.

'I'll know soon enough, I imagine,' said Flora.

'It's Jennifer . . . Jennifer Caird.'

Flora's lips moved, silently repeating the name, almost tasting it. 'How old is she?'

'Oh, Flora,' Duncan said, 'darling.'

'*That* young,' she said. It was a statement, not a question. 'What is she? Blonde? Brunette?' Duncan, unnerved by her quiet persistence and unable to comprehend why she was torturing them both like this, still didn't answer.

'Where did you do it? Her flat? Our flat? The back of a car? Where?'

'Her flat. At least, she said it was.'

'How many times?'

'Oh, Flora, for God's sake, it's over. It hardly even began.'

'When did you do it? In the lunch hour? Waiting for the division bell? When?'

Duncan grabbed Flora and forced her to face him. 'Don't, Flora. Please.'

She took his hands in hers, turned them over, examined them, and said disbelievingly: 'They look the same. Exactly the same.' And then she looked into his eyes. 'And does she cry when she comes – like me?'

'Why are you doing this?' Duncan was genuinely puzzled. 'It – meant – nothing,' he said, spelling it out.

'Yes,' said Flora. 'I see that now.' She turned away from him, her pain unreachable.

The phone rang, startling them both, and Duncan went to the bedside table and picked it up. 'Hello . . . speaking. Oh, how very kind of you to call. She's around somewhere, I think. Hold on a minute, will you . . .' Covering the mouthpiece, he held out the phone to Flora. 'The party chairman's wife?' he said. Flora studied the phone gloomily. Duncan held it out beseechingly. Reluctantly, she crossed the room and took it from him, as he whispered urgently, 'She likes to be called Kitty.'

Apprehensively, Flora put the phone to her ear. 'Hello? Yes, of course I remember . . . oh, adjusting, I suppose . . . trying to come to terms. Yes . . . well, you're very kind, thank you.' She was trying hard to keep control of her emotions and Duncan wanted to hug her for it. 'The next time I'm in town? I'd like that, thank you. Goodbye.' As she hung up, Flora's hands were damp with sweat.

'What did she say?' Duncan asked anxiously.

'They are all counting on me to do the right thing,' said Flora.

Duncan, momentarily relieved, sank onto the bed. 'You do realise, Flora, that there are only two people who count in all this. Those two children across the landing.'

Flora, on her way to the bathroom, turned and looked at him. Something in her face made Duncan decide that this was not a wise line to pursue.

Returning with her sponge-bag and a towel, Flora stuffed them into the second case and closed it. 'I've been doing some counting myself,' she said. 'Counting the times I've signed your letters. Thirty a day for nearly ten years. I make that around seventy-two thousand times I've written "pp Duncan Matlock".' She paused, with meaning. ' "Signed in his absence".'

Duncan recognised the implication, and there was a cold hand of dread in his stomach. Going over to Flora, he put his arms around her and then slipped down onto his knees, his face buried in her skirt. 'Do you want me to beg?' he said brokenly. 'I'll do it. I'm begging you, Flora. Please, please don't go. Don't do this. Don't destroy everything now. I beg you . . .'

Flora touched his head. There was tenderness and sadness in the gesture. Her own humiliation was enough; she couldn't bear to see him kneeling before her. It was a long moment before she could bring herself to speak. 'I'll do whatever is necessary,' she said.

5

Joanna was asleep, breathing deeply. She had quickly come to terms with the fact that they were not, after all, going on holiday.

'When we do go, can Daddy come too?' she'd said.

'I expect so,' Flora had replied, drearily unpacking the cases and putting away Joanna's things, 'if he's not too busy.'

Flora, curled up beside Joanna and unable to sleep, quietly extricated herself from her daughter's bed, padded across the floor and parted the curtains. In the moonlight she could see figures slumped in the Press cars, still parked at the end of her drive. Shivering, she closed the curtains and, fearful of waking anyone else in the house, especially Duncan, went softly downstairs towards the kitchen and a soothing cup of hot chocolate. There was a bulky envelope on the front doormat and Flora stopped, picked it up and examined it. It was unstamped and addressed to 'Mrs Flora Matlock'. She was about to open it when she noticed a light under the study door.

Her father was slumped in an armchair in front of the dying fire. He was wearing the tartan dressing-gown she'd given him last Christmas and there was a half-empty whisky glass in his hand.

'Daddy?' Flora was moved by the tears in his eyes as he turned to look at her.

'I can't believe he's been such a bloody fool, Flora,' he said sadly. 'I just can't believe it.'

'Daddy,' she said again, and, this time, she spoke as though it were a term of endearment. Crossing the room, she knelt at his feet and rested her head on his knee. 'Oh, Daddy.'

'It's more than just a glitch, however you look at it,' Clive said. 'It's a blemish.' Flora noticed a petulant note in his voice. 'Five years . . .' He gazed sorrowfully over his daughter's head at the fire and beyond it. 'I thought maybe ten at the outside, and he'd be the leader. I thought I'd be a part of that – I'd still be young enough.'

Flora lifted up her head and looked at her father as though she was seeing him clearly for the first time. Now, she understood that his tears were not for her. So that's why you wanted me to marry Duncan, she thought, I was just a stepping-stone to power. She didn't voice the thought, because she and her father were unused to telling each other the truth about important things. She turned from him, picked up the poker and prodded the fire. Unhappy, vicious stabs.

'Surely people are more tolerant now?' Clive seemed unaware of the effect of his words. 'More liberal? I mean, its all a bit *déjà vu*, isn't it? After the litany of ligatures, and so forth. Maybe,' he added bracingly, 'there'll be another royal toe-sucking episode and we'll be relegated to the back pages.' He drained his glass. 'Don't mind me, Flo. Just the ramblings of a silly old fool with delusions of adequacy. Ah, well.' He stood up and stretched. 'We'd better get some rest if we're to be ready for the fray.'

He touched her hair awkwardly on the way to the door. 'You're making a bloody fine fist of this, Flora. God knows where you get your strength.'

Left alone, Flora gazed miserably into the fire, and then unbuttoned her cotton nightgown and stared critically down at her body in the firelight, as if seeing it from a new and brutal perspective. Her skin seemed somehow greyer, the stretch-marks more pronounced. As she looked down, she caught sight of the envelope on the floor beside her and opened it. Inside was an audio tape. There was no card or letter.

Puzzled, she buttoned her nightgown and, carrying the tape, crept upstairs and into Paul's room. He was asleep in the top of the bunk-bed, his Sony Walkman still looped around his neck. Flora gently disentangled the Walkman and earphones and slid into the lower bunk. Taking out Paul's tape, she put in her own and put on the earphones.

A woman's voice she didn't recognise was speaking: 'Where are you?'

A man's voice – Duncan's: 'In the study. She's upstairs with the kids.'

The woman's voice again. Flora realised it must be Jennifer: 'God, be careful, Duncan.'

Duncan: 'It's okay, she can't hear . . . Jesus, Jenny, last night was . . .'

Their voices were muted, intimate. Flora, lying in the dark, didn't want to hear any more, but was unable to stop herself listening.

'Was what?'

'It was like standing on the edge of a fucking precipice.'

Jennifer giggled. 'Literally.'

'Did I hurt you?'

'No, no. I was afraid it was the other way around, my darling.'

There was a short silence. Paul stirred in his sleep above Flora, who, terribly still, continued to listen.

Duncan's voice: 'If I close my eyes, I can still taste you.'

'Yes?'

'Oh, yes.'

'Then close them.'

'Oh, no Jenny. Dear God, not now.'

'Yes, now. Hold it for me Duncan. Put your hands there and hold it. Can you feel me? Feel my mouth around you? Feel my tongue on you?'

'Oh, sweet Jesus . . .'

Flora snapped off the tape. This was Duncan, her husband, the man she thought she knew. Her pain was like a scald inside her. Reluctantly, but unable to help herself, she turned on the tape again and, feeling that she was sullying her son's Walkman, readjusted the earphones.

It was Jennifer's voice again. 'Now I'm turning around. I'm turning around on all fours like you wanted. A bitch on heat. I'm raised, waiting for you . . . arched, waiting for you . . .'

'Oh, Christ. Oh, Jesus Christ!'

'Now you're there. Pushing to get inside me . . .'

'Oh, God help me.'

'But I'm tight. . . I'm very tight. . . you have to force your way in. . . push your way in.' Duncan moaned. 'Aah. . . yes. Yes! You're there! You made it! You're inside. . .' There was another pause. 'You're home . . .'

Flora, weeping silently, turned off the tape. One of Paul's hands flopped down over the side of the bunk and, suddenly yearning for human contact, Flora reached out and held it.

Paul was in the utility room, cleaning his shoes for school. He was fascinated by the comings and goings in the kitchen next door. The sort of pompous, navy-blue-suit-and-matching-tie man he would have expected to see sitting on the platform at school speech-days had just burst through a hole in the hedge and was sprinting in through the kitchen door, carrying a pile of newspapers. Paul's father, in pyjamas and dressing-gown, was waiting anxiously at the door. 'Have you got them, Roger?'

'Front page in the *Mail*, the *Express*, the *Sun*, the *Star* and

Today.' Roger dumped the papers on the table. 'The qualities are holding fire, barely a few lines.'

Paul was pleased to observe his grandfather cooking sausages on the Aga, an unexpected bonus, and surprised to see a stranger, a grey-faced man in a dressing-gown (so, he stayed the night, too?) sitting at the table, checking something.

'One banger or two, Mark?' said Clive.

'Two, why not?' Mark pushed the schedule to one side and moved the crockery to make room for the newpapers.

Paul, peering around the door, could just make out newspaper headlines and pictures. MINISTER FOR THE FAMILY AND ESCORT GIRL . . . There was a blurred picture and underneath, 'She posed as a House of Commons Researcher'. Another picture showed a front door. 'The Love-Nest', and below a great big headline, THE FAMILY HE BETRAYED. Paul recognised the photograph of his mum and dad, Joanna and himself taken by a local photographer the day Dad got promoted to Minister. Creeping into the kitchen, he looked over at the papers on the table. SCOUNDREL!. . . IN FLA-GRANTE. . . MORE TORY DIRTY LINEN.

'Shit,' his father said 'They've all got it.'

'Check out the dates, that's still our best angle,' said the pompous man in the navy-blue suit.

Another, much older man came bounding in, wearing a track-suit. 'What's the tally?' he said.

'Not as bad as we thought, Sir Donald,' said Mark.

'Then our hard work must have paid off,' said Sir Donald.

Keeping an eye on the huddle of men, Paul sneaked over to his grandfather and helped himself to a sausage. Somebody said, 'Are the dates an issue?' and the man in the blue suit said: 'We need blatant inaccuracies to trigger the Press Complaints Commission.'

Paul was puzzled. What was going on? Everyone seemed

sort of excited, like the day the exam results were posted up, and yet it sounded . . . horrible. He went over to the bread bin, helped himself to two slices of bread and wrapped them around the sausage.

Suddenly, Duncan caught sight of Paul. 'Upstairs. Now,' he said, in a voice Paul had learned to obey. On his way to the door, he passed the group of men. One of them, the man in the track-suit, ruffled Paul's hair in a well-intentioned sort of way. He wanted to shout, 'Get off, go away, all of you,' but he just jerked his head away tersely, and ran out of the room.

'He's at that age, I'm afraid,' Duncan apologised.

'Weren't we all?' said Sir Donald.

The men grinned ruefully and returned to the papers.

'A brief fling, we can sell as a *crime passionale*,' said Sir Donald. 'But ten months . . . they'll be over us like a rash.'

'Then God help all of us,' said Roger. 'Wait a minute, though. The tapes and pictures only relate to the last month. What's the *Star* got?'

'Duncan grabbed the *Star*. 'The same.'

'Ditto *Today*,' said Sir Donald.

'And the *Sun*,' said Clive.

Mark checked through the papers quickly. 'I count only three direct quotes from the phone-bug.'

'Four. The *Sun*'s got one too,' said Roger.

'Unless the bastards are holding the rest back,' Duncan said. 'To keep the story alive?'

'Not if we've covered all the bases,' said Sir Donald.

Clive plonked a plate of sausages in the centre of the table. 'If a month is all they've got, surely that's all he need admit to?'

'Better yet, a couple of nights,' said Roger. 'Put the rest down to Chinese whispers.'

Sir Donald closed his newspaper and speared a sausage. 'I think I see a frail chink of light, my friends,' he said.

Flora came downstairs, ghostly and pale, supporting herself on the curved banister rail. From the study she could hear a loud and arrogant Home Counties voice, which she recognised as Roger Graveley's: '. . . seen them all, bloody hypocrites. It's prayers in the House and then how soon can they get a leg over some dolly bird. And not a thought for their poor wives.'

Flora winced, turned away from the voices and went off towards the kitchen, just as Sir Donald was leaving it with a sheaf of newspapers under his arm. They could both hear another, quieter voice. 'Come now, Roger,' Mark was saying, 'dolly birds were extinct by the seventies. And as for the wives . . . a man in the grip of passion isn't thinking of his wife, he's thinking of his lover .'

Sir Donald decided to pretend he hadn't heard anything. 'Flora, my dear girl.' He attempted to lead her into the kitchen, away from the voices, but she was gazing fixedly at the newspapers. Silently, she met his eyes and put out a hand.

Reluctantly, Sir Donald gave her the top paper and followed her into the kitchen. He watched anxiously as she leaned against the Aga and, without expression, read the headlines. Then she turned the page and Sir Donald wished he'd had time to censor the papers before handing them over. This one featured a full-page picture of Jennifer Caird, long-limbed, long-haired and undeniably luscious, lounging around a swimming-pool in the smallest bikini ever made.

So, that's what she looks like, Flora thought. She felt sad and drab and suddenly older. She put a hand to her collar, realising that she had forgotten to pin on the diamond cluster brooch, the badge of office Duncan had given her when he won Carlingham.

Sir Donald took the paper from Flora, closed it and gently folded one of her hands in both of his. 'It's going to be a bumpy few days, Flora, my dear. Are you up to it?' He studied her keenly from under bushy grey eyebrows. 'You may read a lot more things, hear a lot more things which will distress you. You wouldn't be human if they didn't.' Flora didn't speak – she couldn't imagine that she would ever hear anything more distressing than those taped voices in the night. 'Duncan's account of what happened is the truth,' Sir Donald was saying. 'Hang on to that. Never doubt it. It was all over before it even began. Everything else is tabloid bull and rumour-mongering. If that weren't the case, Flora, I wouldn't soil my hands with him. I'd let him stew: we all would.'

Flora stared at him for a long time and then gave a slight smile. Sir Donald, discomfited, hoped it was in appreciation of the stewing of Duncan – but wasn't there a trace of cynicism playing about her lips? He decided on a different approach. It had occurred to him, over the years, that the staunchest party members were not necessarily the ones standing up in the house going on about 'core values', but the Tory matriarchs in the constituencies reading the riot act about morality: the wives who were often prepared to sacrifice their private lives and their careers to the Conservative cause. 'This is bloody bad timing,' he said, appealing to Flora's loyalty. 'We're being ravaged by publicity-hungry dissidents who think nothing of defying the Leader, the whips, every decent ethic the party ever stood for. They're probably buckling on their armour, even as we speak. They might just take their cue from you, Flora. From your dignity and your forgiveness.'

'What do you want me to do?'

Sir Donald, reassured by her compliance, but slightly disturbed by the odd flatness of her tone, said: 'After the photo-call I want you and Duncan to go to the Association meeting together. Beard the dragon in his lair, as it were. When you're asked for a comment, don't duck it. Don't hide.

Look them straight in the eye. "What determines a Minister's reputation is how he conducts himself in his work." You know the kind of thing. Then go to London for more of the same.'

'What else?'

'Touch him,' said Sir Donald. 'Hold his arm, whenever you can. Don't wait for him to take the initiative. Let them see there's no hint of constraint between you. They'll all be watching out for that.'

Flora was silent. Sir Donald, wishing he could read her mind, gestured at Flora's grey serge stand-by. 'Is that what you plan on wearing?' Flora shrugged her shoulders. 'Something less funereal, perhaps? A splash of colour? A bit of *joie de vivre,* even?'

'I have a condition,' Flora said abruptly.

'Name it,' Sir Donald replied.

'This photo-call. I want no questions from the Press in front of my children.'

'I stipulated a photo-call only. That's understood.'

'And no hounding them. Not at school, here, anywhere. My friends, too.'

'I'll try. But, as you know, my dear, we are dealing with a species who have all the sensitivity of a kerbstone.' Sir Donald smiled at Flora, who didn't smile back. He decided to divert the moment. 'Speaking of which, Flora, I had Jeremy Phipps draft this press statement. I know he'd appreciate any thoughts you might have.'

Handing Flora the statement, he watched guardedly as she read it.

'What does this mean?' Flora said, slowly and deliberately. 'About us having "marital problems"?'

Quickly retrieving the paper, Sir Donald said: 'Now, let me tell you my thinking on that, Flora . . .'

Closing her eyes, Flora could see two naked bodies on the

rug in front of the study fire. The bodies were hers and Duncan's. They were lovingly entwined, embracing with familiar, seductive ease. 'Oh, no,' She controlled her emotions with difficulty. 'I am not taking the blame for any of this.'

'There's bound to be some malicious tittle-tattle,' Sir Donald said placatingly. 'Sometimes it's best to take the initiative. Make a pre-emptive strike, so to speak.'

'We made love, last weekend, on the rug in front of the study fire,' said Flora, looking straight at Sir Donald. 'Or was that pre-emptive, too?'

Sir Donald was too much of an old hand to show that he was disconcerted. He put a paternal arm around her shoulders. 'Duncan has always hankered for the front line,' he said. 'He thinks that's where the power is, that it will make him invincible. It won't, Flora. *Real* power is invisible, inviolate. You hold his future in the palm of your hand, my dear.' He turned her to face him. 'That's power, believe me. Real power. Only a fool would throw that away.'

6

'So, it's Sheila Hancock this week, then.' Donnie was studying his research notes. 'It says here she's married to John Thaw.'

'Of course she's married to John Thaw,' said Allie. 'Everyone knows that. Coffee, anyone? Phil?'

'Thanks,' said Phil. 'Now Donnie . . .'

'Hang about,' said Donnie, looking up at the television screen which dominated the open-plan office where *Face the Famous* were planning their next programme. 'Looks like a bit of juice.'

On the screen was a large photograph of a sexy-looking girl and a slightly smaller picture of an unpleasant man in a sharp suit. 'Their meetings took place at a penthouse flat in Pimlico belonging to Miss Caird's former boyfriend Alistair Drummond, who claims he installed the security camera and telephone-bug for business reasons,' the presenter was saying.

'Here comes Drummond now,' said Phil. 'Stand by for the high moral tone, everybody.'

Alistair Drummond walked into view, carrying a brief-case and looking pleased with himself. 'He's the Minister for the Family, right?' he said to a group of waiting reporters. 'He's always going on about the value of the family. But how much value does he put on his own family? It's sheer hypocrisy. I think the public have every right to know about it.'

The reporters jostled. 'So, you weren't paid for the story . . . ? Did she work for your escort agency . . . ?'

'No comment as Mr Drummond exits in his very nice silver Merc,' said Donnie. 'I'm in the wrong job, folks.'

'You know who they're talking about, don't you?' said Allie, coming back with the coffee. 'Minister for the Family, that's Flora Matlock's husband . . . you know, the other day . . .'

'What price commitment and basic morality, then?' said Donnie. 'Just another libidinous porker MP getting his end away.'

'What if she doesn't know it's plastered all over the television?' Allie was ferreting in a drawer for the address book. 'It would be terrible if she didn't know.'

'Not our business, love,' said Phil.

Allie looked at him reproachfully. 'She was nice, Mrs Matlock. I'm going to give her a ring.'

In Duncan's Whitehall office Ian Ruby-Smith and Colin Fletcher were also watching the television and listening intently to the news-reader.

'House of Commons research passes are subject to strict security rules and issued only on the recommendation of individual MPs.' The news-reader turned and made an elaborate hand gesture at a large wall monitor behind her, which featured a crusty old Tory backbencher.

'It's Gordon Naylor,' said Ian. 'The old fool.'

'There goes the phone again,' said Colin. 'Shouldn't we . . . ?'

'Ignore them,' said Ian. They both turned back to the screen. Gordon Naylor was now being interviewed.

'Mr Naylor, were you aware that Miss Caird worked for an escort agency?' said the interviewer.

'No, I was not,' Gordon Naylor replied firmly from his

monitor screen. 'She came highly recommended, with a degree, research experience and all the usual references.'

'Plus she had a pretty face and a cute little ass,' said Ian.

'And a degree in aromatherapy?' said Colin.

Flora had taken off the grey serge. She was lying on her bed in her slip. Her television was on, too, but she was not listening to the presenter ('. . . recently worked for Drummond's Escort Agency, run by her former boyfriend, Alistair Drummond. Its clients are said to include prominent Members of Parliament, the legal profession and several leading sporting and pop personalities . . .'). She was looking at Jennifer Caird, emerging from a block of flats to face the Press, with her solicitor by her side. She was wearing a silk shirt, a well-cut black suit, her long hair was blowing in the breeze, and she looked, to Flora's eyes, quite lovely.

The solicitor stepped forward. 'Miss Caird has prepared a statement which I will now read.' As he spoke, the camera and Flora Matlock continued to concentrate on Jennifer Caird. 'What happened between Mr Duncan Matlock and myself is private and between us alone. I only knew our phone conversations were being recorded by Mr Drummond after the event and I utterly condemn his actions. It was not my intention to hurt Mr Matlock or his family.' Jennifer's expression was sweet and sincere and Flora would have liked to kill her. 'But,' the solicitor continued, 'if we hadn't cared deeply for each other we would never have entered the relationship in the first place.'

Flora's face was clenched and rigid as she rose, snapped off the television and went to her wardrobe. She took out a blue floral dress, held it up against herself, and then caught sight of another one – the luminous, bright-red dress she'd bought at Chic a few months ago and which she had been saving for a special occasion.

47

Normally it took Flora only a couple of minutes to do her face. A dab of foundation, a swift brush of translucent powder, maybe a dab of lipstick and a flick of mascara. Today, she stood before the bathroom mirror taking her time, grooming herself for battle.

She was just applying a firm slash of vivid red lipstick when the telephone went and the answering machine snapped into action. 'Flora, it's Charlotte. Sarah's with me . . . we just wanted to say . . . how bloody awful all this is for you . . .' Her voice was excited, highly charged. 'My dear, what on earth was he thinking of?' There were busy background whispers. Flora wasn't listening; she was carefully brushing mascara onto her lashes. 'Sarah says she looks an absolute bimbo. And that truly terrible suit . . .'

Leaning over, Flora flushed the loo and drowned Charlotte before she could say, 'Well, I did warn you . . .'

Wondering who else might be lurking in her answerphone, Flora went into the bedroom and pressed the playback button. Instantly an all-too-familiar robust voice boomed out at her. 'Veronica Weston, Mrs Matlock. Conservative Christian Wives Association? Just wanted to say that our thoughts and prayers are with you at this difficult time, my dear. Many of us have suffered as you are suffering, but through forgiveness and God's help, we have pulled through. As we know you will. God bless you.'

Flora grimaced as she put on the red dress. And then a voice she didn't recognise came on the machine: 'Mrs Matlock? It's me, Alison Sissons, Allie from *Face the Famous*? I really don't want to intrude or anything, but we wondered if you knew . . . it's all on the television now, about your husband. Maybe you'd better take a look. Oh . . . and I've been going through the schedules. Jennifer Caird is down to appear on *Hello and Good Morning* at 11 o'clock. Anything we can do, you've got our number. Bye.'

Flora smoothed the red dress over her hips and approved her reflection in the long wardrobe mirror. That, she said to herself, is probably the only altruistic thing anybody has said to me in the past twelve hours.

Sir Donald couldn't believe his eyes. Coming down the stairs was a strikingly attractive woman in a bright red dress. It was Flora. The first thing he noticed was her body – the dress fitted where it touched – and he wondered idly why such an agreeable shape had previously always been camouflaged in bulky skirts and jumpers. The second thing he noticed was a new and shimmering intensity about her. He was reminded of those films he used to enjoy on sixpenny Saturday mornings at the Odeon when he was a child, where the plain typist falls in love, takes off her spectacles, fixes her hair and turns into Rita Hayworth. 'My dear . . .' He stepped forward and put out a hand.

Duncan stared in amazement. Even on good days, Flora never looked this good, and when he'd left her yesterday evening she'd been a wreck, poor love, totally washed out.

'Is it time?' Flora said, taking Sir Donald's hand.

'Just waiting for the off,' Sir Donald said.

'Mummy, Mummy.' Joanna ran over to Flora. 'Look, I'm wearing my new party dress, too.'

'You look lovely, darling,' said Flora. 'Now, you go and stand between your father and Grandad, and Paul, you come next to me.' Flora put one arm around Paul, whose unyielding body gradually relaxed against her, and her other arm through Duncan's. Lined up by the front door, everyone except for Joanna, who was revelling in all the unaccustomed excitement, looked as though they were bracing themselves for a firing squad.

Mark opened the front door. 'They're ready,' he said.

The family stepped out – Flora looking as though she

49

couldn't remember when she'd had such a good time, Duncan smiling gravely beside her.

The children blinked in the glare of rows and rows of camera lights and flash guns. 'Over here, Mrs Matlock,' one of the photographers shouted. 'How about the kids in front?' said another. 'Look at me, Mrs Matlock . . . Mr Matlock!'

Flora and Duncan turned this way and that, as directed. Then, apparently on impulse, Flora stood on tiptoe and kissed Duncan's cheek. Duncan smiled at her tenderly, put his arm around her, and then swung Joanna up into his arms. There was admiration in Clive's eyes as he looked at his daughter, radiant and composed. Good girl, she really *was* making a fist of it.

'Well, that's that,' Flora said, as they straggled back into the hall. She had stopped smiling, but was still composed and in charge. 'Now,' – she put her arms around Paul and Joanna – 'you two run upstairs and get into your school things. Mrs Lucas has kindly offered to take you.'

'Why can't you take us to school?' said Paul.

'Daddy and I have to go out . . .'

'I want to come, too,' said Joanna, who thought this was all a lot more fun than Nature with Miss Birney.

'No, off you go,' said Flora. 'I'll come and pick you both up this afternoon. Promise.'

Over at the BBC, discussions on the Sheila Hancock interview had come to a standstill. The *Face the Famous* team remained riveted to the television, watching events unfold outside the Carlingham Conservative Association HQ. 'That's not her, the politician's wife.' said Phil.

'Flora Matlock. Yes it is,' said Allie. 'Getting out of the car now. Doesn't she look amazing?'

'So that's the errant husband,' said Donnie, as Duncan

stepped out behind Flora, took her arm and hurried her into the building. 'Not a bad-looking bloke, actually.'

A reporter, standing outside the HQ, was saying: 'Duncan Matlock hasn't yet made a full statement on the affair. It's believed that will come when he makes his speech at a long-standing dinner engagement at the Family Policy Forum . . .'

'That'll be a tricky one,' said Donnie. 'And I don't fancy his chances with that fearsome female getting out of the Austin Princess over there. Just driven in from the Tory heartlands, I'd say, powered by moral indignation.'

'Mrs Rosalind Clegg, the vice chairman of the Association, has now arrived,' the reporter said. 'Recent events have shown us – with both Mrs Horrigan and Mrs Fitzpatrick – that local party activists carry more than a little influence in these controversies. Will Mrs Clegg follow in their footsteps?' She thrust her microphone in front of Mrs Clegg. 'Mrs Clegg, will you be asking for Mr Matlock's resignation at the meeting?'

Mrs Clegg stopped, squared her shoulders and thinned her lips. 'I will only say this. There are those of us in the Association who believe that the private conduct of a Minister has a bearing on his public position. I'm afraid that is all I am prepared to say at this time.'

'Poor bugger,' said Phil, as Rosalind Clegg bustled, self-importantly, into the building. 'It's serious come-into-my-study time, isn't it?'

'It seems that it may well be here, in Carlingham, at the local Conservative Headquarters, that Duncan Matlock's fate, and that of his Ministry, will ultimately be decided,' the reporter said.

'Well, watch this space,' said Phil.

An hour later, Flora and Duncan Matlock, looking pale and drawn, came out of the Conservative headquarters.

Reporters flurried around them and Flora blinked in the glare of flashlights and cameras.

'Oh, poor Mrs Matlock,' said Allie.

'Ssh,' said Phil, 'that reporter, over there by the lamp post, he's just asked Duncan Matlock if he's had to resign.'

Duncan, putting his arm round Flora and drawing her closer to him, was saying: 'It was a constructive meeting, where diverse views were aired and considered. The Executive is still sitting and will make a statement in due course.'

'Did Mrs Clegg voice an opinion?' one of the reporters called out.

'I'll bet she did,' said Donnie.

'Did you speak in support of your husband, Mrs Matlock?' shouted another reporter.

In a clear voice, Flora said: 'I'm confident that the Association – and the public in general – will judge my husband by how he does his job. Not a momentary indiscretion in his private life. Thank you.'

'Sounds as if she's reading a script,' said Donnie. 'I wonder who wrote it?'

They watched as Duncan hustled Flora into a car. 'Oh, look at her face,' said Allie. 'She's like a ghost.'

7

Flora hated the Civic Centre hall where Duncan held his weekly surgery – or, more often, where she held Duncan's weekly surgery.

She hated the empty desolation of it. The hard chairs ranged unwelcomingly around the walls and the chipped grey and green institutional paintwork. But, most of all, she hated not being able to do anything for the people who came for help. Some of them, of course, were born whingers, but most had genuine grievances. Like Margot and Suzie, who had been fighting unsuccessfully for months to keep open a much-needed day nursery.

She'd hoped to avoid surgery this morning – she didn't think she could face any more sympathy after the ordeal at Tory HQ, all those heads tilted around concerned smiles – but Sir Donald had been insistent.

'Business as usual,' he'd said firmly. 'You and Duncan did a good job at Headquarters; now you've got to nurture the grassroots, show the party workers and your constituents that you're rock solid and confident.'

Flora had changed back into her grey serge, to match the Centre's decor, and now they were once again being forced to run the full gamut of reporters and cameramen to get into the building. As they dashed inside, one of the younger, fitter party workers slammed the bolts on the doors behind them. 'Sorry about the ruckus, everyone,' said Duncan, tugging off his coat and throwing it on one of the chairs. 'Thanks for turning out. We appreciate the support.'

There was a polite murmur from the mostly middle-aged women who were shifting tables and chairs around in preparation for the business ahead. A table and two chairs were placed in the centre of the room for Flora and Duncan, with two chairs in front for the constituents. The woman organising tickets for the order of entrance had settled herself at a table by the inner door.

Somebody put a stack of papers in front of them, somebody else started handing round coffee and biscuits.

'Shall we get to it, ladies?' Duncan rubbed his hands together to suggest action.

'Number one, please,' called out the party worker with the tickets.

'I'll need the usual prompting, my darling,' Duncan whispered to Flora.

Flora didn't reply. Although she'd had to smile a lot at Duncan during the last couple of hours, she had not exchanged more than two words with him since the previous evening. She wrote swiftly on a piece of paper, 'Local nursery – no funds', and pushed it over to Duncan. He rose and greeted four women with wild hair who were wearing grubby jeans, sweatshirts and dungarees and carrying assorted toddlers. 'Morning, Mrs Matlock,' said one of the women, ignoring Duncan's outstretched hand.

'Hello, Margot,' said Flora. Margot looked dishevelled, but she was, as Flora had discovered, precise in her thinking.

'How are we on chairs?' Duncan looked around for somebody to produce two more. 'Well, hello there.' He bent down and ruffled the hair of one of the toddlers. 'And what's your name?'

The toddler, who was black and stocky, stared back at him without answering.

'Justin,' said Margot.

'A real little John Barnes in the making,' said Duncan.

Nobody responded to this, either. The women, who now all had chairs, sat and gazed at Duncan blankly, shooting occasional sympathetic glances at Flora, who forced herself to meet their eyes.

'So what's the latest on the funding problem?' said Duncan.

'We reapplied to the Council, like you suggested . . .' Margot said, looking at Flora.

'And got precisely nowhere,' said Suzie, who was fatter, untidier and older than Margot.

'Did you raise the special needs aspect?' Flora asked.

Suzie grimly handed over a letter from the Council: 'The lease is up at the end of the month. Thirty children will get turfed out – which means thirty working women will have to quit their jobs to look after them.'

'And most of them are the sole breadwinners – single parents,' said Margot.

'Well now . . .' Duncan sat back in his chair and fiddled with a pencil. 'How about some fund-raising of your own? A kiddies' play? Custard pies and candy-floss? Make them smile while they reach for their cheque books.'

'We're talking over £21,000,' said Suzie.

'Farting about with candy-floss won't even make a dent in it,' said Margot.

Duncan looked at her coldly and said, with a dismissive nod: 'I'll get on to the Council myself, see if I can't get it raised at committee level.'

'Those kids and their families depend on us,' Suzie said.

'Right.' Duncan got up and extended his hand. 'I'll deal with it personally. Thank you so much for finding the time to come and see me.'

As the women and children straggled out, Margot went over to Flora and, looking at her searchingly, reached into a carrier bag and produced a wilted bunch of wild flowers.

Holding them out to Flora, she said: 'We picked these for you. The kids made their own garden, at the nursery.'

'Thank you.' Flora took them and put them down carefully on the table next to her. She hoped she wasn't going to cry.

Duncan tossed the Council letter casually onto a pile of paperwork, glanced at the flowers and murmured, 'God, the lengths people will go to to get what they want, eh?' He nodded over to the ticket woman by the door. 'Okay, keep 'em coming, ladies!'

Slumped in the back of the Ministry car, Duncan looked at Flora and said: 'Not too bad, so far? What do you think?'

'Nothing,' Flora replied.

'Do you want to stop off and pick up some lunch? You haven't eaten anything since yesterday.'

'No,' said Flora.

They pulled into the drive. Ignoring Duncan, Flora jumped out and went straight into the kitchen, where Mrs Lucas was stirring a big pan of home-made soup. 'It's like feeding the five thousand, Mrs Matlock,' she said. 'Can I get you anything? You look really done in.'

Flora sniffed the aroma of chicken and vegetables. 'A bowl of soup would be nice,' she said. 'Thank you.'

'You go and lie down,' said Mrs Lucas, 'I'll bring it up to you.'

In the bedroom, Flora studied the video recorder in the corner as though it were an enemy. Inside it was the Jennifer Caird interview. She was too tired to face that now. Taking off her shoes and dress, she fell into bed, and was almost asleep when Mrs Lucas tapped at the door and came in with the tray.

'I've heated up a couple of rolls as well,' she said, 'and

there's some nice fresh orange juice, and coffee in the thermos.'

'Thank you, Mrs Lucas,' Flora said. 'This evening . . . I wondered . . . would you be able to read to Joanna?'

'No problem,' said Mrs Lucas. 'It's *The Secret Garden* again, isn't it? I always like that.' As she was going out of the door she turned back and said: 'Mrs Matlock? I just wanted you to know. We're all rooting for you.'

It was 3.45 by the time Flora woke up and remembered that she'd promised to collect the children from school. Flinging on dress and shoes, flicking her hair with a comb and her face with a flannel, she dashed downstairs and bumped into Mark Hollister.

'Can't stop,' she said. 'I've got to collect Joanna and Paul.'

'You'd better let me drive you,' said Mark. 'The Press may be staked out. Which one first?'

'St Mary's,' said Flora.

The only crowd outside St Mary's was the usual gathering of mothers, gossiping together in the playground. Flora suspected she knew what the gossip was about today. She waved at Joanna, who ran over and jumped into the back of the car.

'Gillian Greene said Daddy was on television this morning,' she said. 'Her mummy switched it off before she could watch it.'

Flora looked at Mark. 'Members of Parliament are on television all the time, Joanna,' he said.

Rounding the corner into the drive of Carlingham College, he suddenly put his foot down on the accelerator pedal. 'Hold on,' he said. 'I'm going to drive on through them.'

'What's going on?' Joanna peered excitedly out of the window. A swarm of reporters was pushing its way through clusters of parents to get to the car.

Mark pulled up right outside the front door, opened the passenger door and said: 'Go for it.'

Flora jumped out and was inside the school before the reporters could get to her. She found Paul waiting in the lobby with Mr Pearson, his housemaster.

'There's another way out the back, Mrs Matlock,' Mr Pearson said. 'Follow me.'

The route brought Flora and Paul out through a group of parents, who stepped aside to make way for them. Flora could feel their curious gaze on her back as she rushed through, dragging Paul after her.

'There she is!' A reporter spotted them and was instantly joined by the others.

'How do you see the future, Mrs Matlock?'

'You're definitely going to stand by your husband, are you, Mrs Matlock?'

'Was it an easy decision to make?'

'When did he tell you about the affair, Mrs Matlock?'

'Come on, darling.' Flora grabbed Paul closer to her and pushed her way through the throng.

'Is it true your husband offered to resign over the affair?'

'How are the kids holding up, Mrs Matlock?'

Mark Hollister was ready for them. He had the rear door open and was holding back the reporters. Flora bundled Paul towards Joanna and dived in beside him.

'Right, we're off.' The car's engine was still turning over. Mark slammed his foot down hard and they zigzagged out of the quadrangle. All the way down the drive, reporters' faces pressed against the windows, clamouring and shouting. Cameras popped and flashed.

Flora saw her children huddling back, white-faced and scared, and her whole body was suddenly charged with fierce anger.

Paul felt like a stranger in his own home. Coming down to the kitchen to wheedle some toast and Marmite out of Mrs Lucas, he found, instead of her familiar figure tending the Aga or putting out biscuits for Basker, the grey-faced man in the queer shades, who he now knew to be Mark, the seriously dangerous driver. He was prowling around the place, talking tensely into his mobile, and the kitchen table was littered with papers and files, like a command post.

'Keep me posted will you?' he was saying. 'No, the local party is still in session . . . Right, okay, do that.'

Paul stood in the doorway and watched Mark press the off-switch and then rapidly redial. He wondered whether he ought to cough or something, to show that he was about to cross the kitchen to the larder on his Marmite hunt, but by the time he'd decided he probably should, Mark was rapping keenly again. 'Some bloody loose-lips from the Twenty-two Committee was on *P.M.* today, Jeremy Phipps heard it, just called me . . . Oh, the usual . . . "personal admiration but a lot of people will be very disappointed", etc. This thing is going to snowball. I can feel it in my water . . .'

Paul noticed the gleam behind Mark's glasses: excited, but sort of sneaky. He shivered. There was a chill in the air.

'He starts speaking at 8.30, directly after dinner,' Mark went on. 'Tell them we want full media coverage . . . sure they'll buy it, they're wetting themselves in case he cancels . . . oh, hold it . . .' Mark noticed Paul in the doorway and clapped a hand over the mouthpiece. 'Don't mind me, Paul. Anything I can do for you?' Removing his hand from the mouthpiece, he continued speaking. 'Sorry about that . . . no, it's all right. Duncan's kid was hanging about, but he seems to have disappeared.'

Paul felt a bit sick. He'd gone right off the Marmite idea. What he'd really have liked was a perfectly normal afternoon. Tea in the kitchen with Mum and Jo and Mrs Lucas, a

'I'm trying to,' Flora said.

They sat there for a bit with their arms around each other. And then Paul said: 'Does that mean I have to?'

'It might help if you did,' Flora said gently.

Paul's voice was dead, without feeling, as he recited: 'Forgive those who trespass against us?'

He felt his mother's arms tighten around him. There was something odd about the way she continued: 'And lead us not into temptation.' As if, Paul thought, she felt that somehow *she* was being led into temptation.

Joanna and Paul – still wan-faced, but partially revived by a short dose of *Star Trek* – were now watching *Top of the Pops*. Flora, who had sat through the cartoons and ten minutes of loud noise and frenzied movement, slipped upstairs to the bedroom to watch her own television.

She slipped a cassette into the video, wedged a chair under the door-handle, and hit rewind.

She pressed the switch and was immediately faced by morning television's relentlessly cheery husband-and-wife team, John and Angie.

'Hello and good *morn*ing.' Angie beamed at John and then at the camera. 'With us in the studio today is Jennifer Caird, centre of this morning's Press revelations . . .'

John beamed back at Angie, elbowing forward to get his share of the introduction – 'who is going to talk to us *exclusively* about her affair with Duncan Matlock, Minister for the Family.'

Jennifer Caird was sitting on the guest sofa opposite Angie and John. She was still wearing the same discreet, well-cut suit, and – Flora got some small satisfaction from this – looked rather nervous.

'Pretty torrid stuff to read over the breakfast table, Jennifer?' said Angie matily.

'They print whatever comes into their heads, don't they?' replied Jennifer.

'Are you saying, then, that the substance of the story isn't true?' said John, who obviously fancied himself as the hard-nosed investigative half of the duo.

'If you print anything out of context it loses its veracity, don't you think?'

Angie and John nodded, clearly impressed by Jennifer's intelligent, direct replies.

'The references, for example, to Mr Matlock's sexual preferences – that he likes a woman to dominate him in bed – this was a direct quote from you, was it not?' Angie said. 'To a close friend?'

Jennifer, now totally confident, said: 'Successful men often like to be disempowered in the sexual act. There's nothing new about that. Particularly if their wives are passive or sexually unadventurous.'

Flora sank onto the bed where her children were conceived, where she and Duncan had happily, uninhibitedly made love for so many years. She gazed at the screen in disbelief. It was such a cruel betrayal. She knew, whatever happened, that she would never again trust Duncan – or any other man, for that matter.

'Yet you claim your relationship was based on more than just sex?' said John.

Jennifer achieved a smile both demure and knowing. 'Sex is a demonstration of love, isn't it?' she said. 'The more passionate the love, it follows the more intense the sex. For a woman that's how it is, anyway.'

'And for Duncan Matlock?' Angie asked.

'You'll have to ask him that.'

'But as an escort girl you were presumably paid for your services?' There was a trace of asperity in Angie's tone. 'Well paid?'

'That's entirely different.' Jennifer was in charge now, apparently unfazed by the question. 'And it's in the past,' she added firmly. 'I haven't worked for Drummond's for nearly a year. Duncan Matlock never paid me. He entered our relationship voluntarily and willingly, just as I did. We were talking about spending the rest of our lives together.'

Flora, shivering, cold as ice, watched the drama unfold on the screen as though it had nothing to do with her. She was breathing deeply and rhythmically, determined not to let this get to her.

'You mean,' said John, 'that he was planning to divorce his wife in order to marry you?'

'I mean exactly that,' Jennifer said. 'It was only half a marriage, anyway. He said he and his wife were more like brother and sister than man and wife . . .'

Flora abruptly switched the tape off. For a long time she remained sitting on the bed, bathed in the haze of the early evening dusk.

8

It was midnight, and Flora was lying in bed listening to Duncan moving about their bathroom, making familiar teeth-cleaning noises. Since all the spare beds were full, she'd hoped he would make up a bed in the study, but here he was, and she was too tired now to turn him out, to argue or remonstrate.

As he drew back the covers and crawled into bed beside her, she moved away, turning her back to him. He snuggled up behind her. 'Like spoons,' they used to say.

Putting an arm around Flora's waist, Duncan said: 'Patterson just checked in. They've adjourned for the night. He says that bloody Clegg woman is stuffed with more hormones than a Christmas turkey. She's like a dog with a bone, won't give up.'

Flora didn't trust herself to speak.

'Darling?' Duncan waited a moment, but Flora didn't respond. 'Darling,' he said, 'you're still hurting. I know. I'll make it up to you, my love. Believe me.'

He rolled her over and looked deeply into her eyes. There was an honesty there, a decency which had always moved him. Dear, sweet Flora. He really meant it when he said, 'I've never wanted you more than at this moment. Do you know that?'

She stared at him silently as he slowly, gently started to unbutton her nightdress. And then suddenly, without any premeditation, she was flailing at him, lashing out and row with Jo over what to watch on telly. Even – he could not believe he was thinking this – an hour of maths homework with Mum banging on about decimal points.

Passing the study, he overheard his father's voice. The door was slightly open, and through the crack, Paul saw his father and Sir Donald, the man with the bushy eyebrows, huddled together over a lap-top computer.

'Para three . . . pressure of work,' Sir Donald was saying.

'Sounds a bit limp-fisted, doesn't it?' His father fiddled with the keyboard.

'Yes, you're right. Cut it. Replace it with "an error of judgement, which I bitterly regret . . ." '

'Or . . .' – Paul couldn't understand why his father seemed quite so pleased with himself as he looked up at Sir Donald – 'how about "No one regrets more bitterly than I do . . . "? '

Sir Donald nodded approvingly: 'Better.'

Paul turned and ran upstairs, two at a time.

A few minutes later, Flora, passing the bathroom, caught sight of Paul filling the hand-basin with water. On the floor, next to him, was his Gameboy and a pile of other games and books. Stricken, she watched him methodically plunge them into the water, pressing the Gameboy down again and again.

'Oh, Paul . . .' She moved swiftly into the bathroom and pulled out the plug. 'It was your birthday present.'

Paul's lips were quivering. '*He* didn't choose it, you did.'

'Darling.' Flora sat on the side of the bath and pulled Paul onto her lap. What was it that reporter had said? How are the kids holding up?

Paul was looking at his mother, puzzled. 'How could he?' he said. 'You're so beautiful.'

Flora, who could feel her own lips beginning to tremble, managed a rueful smile.

'Do you forgive him?' Paul asked.

striking him. The force of it took him by surprise. 'Hey! Hey!' he cried out.

Flora was arched like an angry cat, clawing at him with a rage so intense she thought it would consume her. Duncan put up his hands to defend himself and then grabbed her, trapping her arms behind her back.

'Not my face,' he said urgently, releasing her. 'Don't go for my face. Okay?'

He lay back and looked up at her expectantly. It began to dawn on Flora that he was waiting for her to attack him again; that her anger excited him. 'Successful men often like to be disempowered in the sex act . . .' Flora heard the voice, visualised the women in bed with her husband. Disgusted with Duncan and herself, she tried to roll away from him, but he dragged her back. Now, they were rolling over and over in the bed. She silently fought against him, but he overpowered her and, turning her over, mounted her from behind. 'It's all right, my darling,' he whispered in her ear as he entered her. 'We're still a team. I'll never leave you.'

He rose to a climax and Flora lay rigidly still, her mind set against the sensation of him inside her. She was staring fixedly at Margot's wild flowers in the vase next to the bed. Somehow, they consoled and strengthened her.

Duncan slumped onto her, nuzzling her shoulder in gratitude. 'God,' he said, 'that was fantastic. Better than ever before.'

He fell asleep almost immediately, snoring rhythmically. Flora had always found Duncan's ability to drop back on the pillow and instantly fall asleep after sex inexplicably demeaning. She lay there, eyes wide open, hating him, despising herself, physically and emotionally bruised. Was that rape? Charlotte would certainly say it was. But Charlotte was of the 'if she says no she means no' school of thought, even when the women had thrown off her clothes and invited the man eagerly into her bed with a bottle of champagne and a condom.

Flora held the opposite, unfashionable view: that the world was full of women sending out contrary sexual signals, which were then received and acted upon by men who were only very rarely tuned in to emotional matters. She knew that she had not just been raped by her husband, that it could not have happened without her tacit compliance. Goodness knows, Duncan was so desperate for her to act the part of the loyal, loving wife that she could have asked him or denied him anything and he'd have agreed. So, why hadn't she stopped him getting into bed with her? Even banned him from their bedroom altogether? She was tired? True. It was habit? Possibly – they'd been sleeping side by side for twenty years. But somewhere deep in her psyche there was the need to prove that she was a passionate and desirable woman. 'Brother and sister,' Jennifer Caird had said. The words taunted and mocked her. She lay staring into the shadows, trying to collect her scattered thoughts.

Truly, she had felt nothing but abhorrence as she fought Duncan off, but there was no doubt that she had been aroused – by her own fury as much as his passionate violence.

Flora sighed; too much had happened too quickly, her mind was in turmoil, she'd never get to sleep. When Duncan started whistling through his teeth with each exhalation Flora could stand it no longer. Slipping out of bed, she put on her dressing-gown and went quietly down the stairs and into the study. The fire was still glowing comfortingly in the grate. She sat down at Duncan's desk, leant back, and swivelled the chair to and fro. Switching on the anglepoise, she noticed his Ministerial red boxes on the floor beside her. Flora reached out and rested a hand on the boxes. She felt a sudden charge of adrenalin, as if she were touching the source of Duncan's power. She tried the clasp, but it was locked.

Idly, she opened the cigar box. Flora had never smoked; she had never even fancied an illicit puff when her school friends keenly lit up behind the gym. But now she took a slim Panatella out of the box, lit it with the desk lighter, and stared abstractedly at the spiral of smoke eddying above her. She didn't quite know why she was doing this, but it made her feel curiously in control . . . almost the way she'd felt when Duncan had cried out: 'Not my face . . . don't go for my face.'

'. . . Ladies and Gentlemen, on behalf of all those at the Family Policy Forum, I'd like to extend a welcome to our speaker tonight, the Right Honourable Duncan Matlock, Minister for the Family.'

The chairman sat down. Everyone turned towards the high table, where Flora and Duncan were seated, along with various luminaries of the Family Policy Forum. Below them stretched long banqueting tables, tightly packed with men in dinner-jackets and women in glittering evening dresses. They had all eaten an indifferent caterers' meal and were now settling back, expectant, hushed, to await the cabaret, the high spot of the evening. The final destruction, or the remarkable regeneration, of Duncan Matlock. Around the hall, the reporters reached for their notebooks and the cameras swung into action.

Duncan rose to his feet to the strobe of flashlights and a ripple of polite applause. 'What is a family?' he began. 'Is it simply a collection of individuals, bound together by the common tie of blood or legal arrangement?'

Flora, gazing purposefully over the sea of curious and speculative faces, saw Colin Fletcher and Mark Hollister, discreetly watching from a doorway. She gave them a faint smile. Colin was thinking: God, she's a looker; what was he doing messing around with bits on the side? Mark was thinking: There's solid steel behind that delicate, upper-class fragility; I wonder if Duncan knows that?

'Recently I lost my way,' Duncan was saying. 'I made an error of judgement which I bitterly regret and will do until my dying breath. Without the love, understanding and loyalty of my family – particularly my wife – I would be lost indeed.'

The cameras and a hundred pairs of eyes rested on Flora. Behind the dutifully attentive mask she was presenting to the room, she was back at Mindermere with her family. She hadn't wanted to leave the children to come to London. It had been very important to her that she should be at home, representing routine and normality, but Mrs Lucas had assured her that she could cope. Joanna, thank goodness, was no problem. She appeared to have adjusted cheerfully to her father's notoriety and sprung out of school each day on a high of popularity. 'Gillian *and* Carolyn saw Dad on television yesterday,' she'd said, basking in the reflected glory of celebrity. But Paul . . . Flora's heart lurched daily as she watched him cross the quadrangle towards her, a solitary figure, apparently abandoned by his usual group of friends. And he had been unnaturally docile at home. Taking his tea up to his room and settling to his homework without chatting to her or Joanna or Mrs Lucas. Flora would have welcomed even the customary rows: 'No, you can't see *Tomorrow's World* until you've finished your biology . . . because I say so.'

She'd had a word with Mr Pearson, the other day, and he had assured her that although Paul was going through a tricky patch, it would all blow over, the way these things have a habit of doing. 'You know how it is, Mrs Matlock,' he'd said, looking over her left shoulder. 'Boys . . . well, they can be cruel. I'm afraid poor old Paul has had to put up with a certain amount of teasing . . . escort girls and so on . . .' He'd caught her eye briefly then: 'Er, forgive me, Mrs Matlock. We'll keep an eye on him, don't you worry.'

'It was their courage, their forgiveness, their compassion, which made me realise the terrible price I might have paid,' Duncan was saying. Flora perceived that it was the women in particular who seemed to be drinking all this in. 'I learned other things, too. About myself, about the woman I married. About the strength of the union we share. I have learnt that sometimes in life you have to make a shameful and stupid mistake in order to face your own human frailty, and so rediscover your humanity.'

Duncan was talking without notes now, as though he was speaking from the heart. Only Flora – and Jeremy Phipps, sitting across the table from her – knew how long it had taken Duncan and Jeremy to write this speech last week, in the study at Mindermere. How Duncan had learnt every line from tape, honing a nuance here, rehearsing a thoughtful pause there. How it had taken him most of an afternoon to perfect the precisely correct tone and expression for a sincere catch in the throat. And how he had failed to notice that Paul was avoiding him, that he hadn't set eyes on his son for two days.

'I learned from my wife, too,' Duncan was saying, 'that this is no time for cowardice or defeat. I have seen the dark side of the moon. But my wife made me see that I must come out the other side, not cowed, but fighting. Because, above all, I learned that I prize my family beyond all else. The prize is worth any endeavour and every effort to ensure its survival . . .' Flora briefly closed her eyes, a control exercise to stop herself interjecting something inappropriately true and awful. Opening them, she was once again able to resume her expression of rapt admiration at her husband's words. 'I don't just mean my own family, to whom I owe so much. But every family in every street in every town in this still great country of ours. I make a pledge to you now . . .' Duncan was getting into his stride; he could sense the audience warming to him. '. . . I make it with all the vigour of someone who was lost, and who found himself. Of someone who was blinded by conceit, but who came to see clearly once again. I intend to fight to ensure that the family gets priority in Government policy . . .' There was a murmur of approval, and Flora thought she detected a cynical glint behind Mark Hollister's glasses. '. . . I intend to fight to ensure that it takes up its rightful position in the heartland of our legislative process. Because if the salvation of one individual rests upon it, so it does for a nation.' Duncan went out of rhetorical mode and effected a deprecating half-smile which Flora recognised as the curtain-raiser to the choked-up, sincere finale. 'If those of you listening to me tonight can extend the same compassion, the same forgiveness as my own family, I promise you, you will not find me wanting again.'

He sat down. There was silence for a moment, then the rafters echoed with applause. The audience rose to their feet clapping. Duncan stood and gravely acknowledged their approbation. Then he turned and raised Flora to her feet, so that she could share in his moment of triumph.

'Sweetheart,' he whispered in her ear. 'Bless you. Jenkins – he's waiting for us in a black limo outside the front door. I'll have to make my number with a few of the worthies. I'll join you in a minute, okay?'

'Of course,' Flora said.

In the cloakroom she collected compliments along with her coat. 'Positively inspiring . . . please tell your husband how much we enjoyed his speech, Mrs Matlock . . . a well deserved tribute, if I may say so, my dear . . . you must be so proud . . .'

Then she hurried out to the car and, huddled in the back, watched the crowds disperse, talking animatedly and nodding their heads approvingly. Eventually, Duncan appeared with Mark Hollister and Colin Fletcher. Spotting the limo, he broke off and bounded down the steps to talk to her through the window.

'Darling! The 1922 are behind me. We just got a call. If the local party stands solid, I'm home and dry.' Through the dark glass, Flora could sense the vibrancy of his excitement. 'There's a spot on *Newsnight*. I have to whip straight round there. Can you make your own way to the flat?'

'Of course,' Flora said.

Pushing the red boxes into the car beside her, Duncan said, 'Guard these with your life.' And then he reached through the window and cupped her chin lovingly with his hands. 'We might just be turning this thing around, my darling.'

He was unable to see Flora's sombre expression in the darkness of the car, but he guessed she would be smiling back at him. He kissed her lightly and turned to the driver. 'The flat, Jenkins. You know the address.'

'Right you are, sir,' said Jenkins.

9

Flora let herself into the flat and switched on the light. The living-room, its walls covered with family photographs and framed drawings by Paul and Joanna, was immaculately tidy. Flora put the red boxes on the teak sideboard and turned on the mock-coal gas fire and the television. She wandered into the two bedrooms, one of which Duncan used as a study. Again, there was none of his usual mess: no clothes thrown around haphazardly for someone else to pick up, no newspapers and half-empty mugs and glasses littering the floor, no papers scattered over the desk. Flora remembered, years ago, her friend, Sarah, talking about her adulterous husband. 'I always knew that if the flat was tidy, he was having an affair,' she'd said. 'It's a clue, the male equivalent of wives buying sets of lace-trimmed lingerie.'

Flora couldn't remember when she had wanted a drink so badly. Going into the tiny kitchen-diner, she located a bottle of Chablis and a corkscrew, and was about to pull the cork when a familiar voice on the television caught her attention. Leaning in the doorway, still wearing her coat, Flora opened the wine as Hugo Patterson was beamed from the Carlingham HQ, reading a prepared statement. 'We feel we should take our lead from Mrs Matlock; from her steadfastness and her forgiveness . . .' Still wearing her coat, Flora reached for a glass, took a slug of Chablis, and turned back to the television: '. . . and it is the majority view of the committee, therefore, that Duncan Matlock has the calibre to remain serving as our Member of Parliament. We are sure that he will, once again, prove himself worthy of the confidence his wife and ourselves have placed in him. Thank you.'

The Press clamoured around Hugo Patterson. Flora gazed at the scene dispassionately. She felt as if it had nothing to do with her at all. She was surprised by the entry-phone security buzzer. Surely not Duncan? She was not expecting him for hours. Turning down the TV volume, she went to the entry-phone, and was even more surprised when a familiar voice identified himself. She pressed the button to let him in. Dropping her coat in the bedroom, she threw back another gulp of wine and opened the front door.

'I'd say I was passing but it would be a lie.' Mark Hollister walked straight in, dumped his briefcase on the sitting-room floor and nodded towards the bottle of wine in Flora's hand. 'That looks tempting.'

Flora fetched another glass, poured out the wine, and passed the glass to Mark. His hands were shaking as he took it and he knocked it back instantly. He seemed oddly ill at ease. Flora refilled his glass, and they both watched Rosalind Clegg on the television as she bustled, mettlesome and angry, through a group of reporters to her car.

Mark raised his glass to Flora. 'He's won, hasn't he?'

'With a little help from his friends,' Flora said.

Flashing her a slightly questioning look, Mark said: 'Sir Donald says men like Duncan are exempt from the usual codes of conduct, because they make history. They're born to it.'

'Duncan went to a grammar school,' Flora said.

'Yes,' Mark said, 'but he married well.' He believed he saw something complicit in the way she met his eyes. Without any warning, he set down his glass and opened the briefcase. 'I'm going out on a limb here, Flora. I hope to God you don't make me regret it.'

Flora waited, puzzled, as Mark dumped the contents of

the briefcase onto the coffee-table. The photographs, at least a dozen or so, were of Duncan with Jennifer Caird. Some were taken on a beach, others over a candle-lit dinner, several in a car. There were also two audio tapes. Flora stared down at them, and then drained her glass.

'Pull the right strings and it's amazing who will crawl out of the woodwork to dance to the party tune.' Mark looked at Flora, trying to gauge her response.

She reached out, skewed one of the pictures round to look at it, and shivered. She felt tainted, just touching it, 'That tape,' she said, slowly comprehending. 'It was you.'

'The journo who got hold of the story owed Sir Donald a favour,' Mark said. 'I felt you were owed the truth. The dates are on the back.'

Flora turned the pictures over and understood what the dates meant. Something inside her tightened like a fist. 'Sir Donald knows about this?'

'They all know, including your father.' Flora winced involuntarily. 'It lasted the best part of a year. If the Press hadn't rumbled him, he'd still be seeing her. He's infatuated with her.' Flora stood rigidly still, making an effort to control her emotions. Up until then, Mark had been speaking in the matter-of-fact tones of a courier dispassionately delivering goods and a message. Now, there was self-loathing in his voice as he said: 'He spotted her at the party conference. He stalked her. He used me as the go-between. Remember that half-term when he couldn't join you and the kids on the ski trip because of his workload? They were in Antigua the whole week.'

Flora, staring blindly at the pictures, wanted Mark to stop, but needed him to go on.

'When your daughter had a burst appendix, remember? He couldn't get to the hospital because of a three-line whip?'

Mark gestured around the flat. 'They were right here, in this flat, all night.'

'Oh no . . . no.'

'Your birthday, last month,' Mark continued inexorably. 'When he said he couldn't come home because –'

Flora put her hands to her ears. 'All right. Enough.' She turned away from him, trying to compose herself. 'Why are you doing this? Telling me all this?'

Mark looked up and met her eyes. 'There's some graffiti on a wall near my flat. "The urge to destroy is creative." '

Through the mask of his glasses, Flora discerned, for the first time, the envy of the misfit who has never quite made it to the top, suspects he never will and is forced to serve lesser men. There was resentment there, and hate, and it frightened her in a primal, visceral way. She moved past him and flung open the door. 'Go now. Please.'

She had difficulty controlling herself as he picked up his briefcase and walked slowly towards the door. Pausing on the threshold he bowed. 'I'm sorry, Flora. Call it an error of judgment on my part.'

After Mark had left, Flora stood quite still for a moment with her eyes closed, trying to calm herself. Then she picked up one of the tapes and slotted it into the cassette. It was another recorded conversation between that woman and her husband. This time, Jennifer Caird was on her mobile phone and Duncan was, it appeared, calling from his office.

'But you're on your mobile,' Duncan was saying.

'Yes,' Jennifer replied, 'but I'm here, at your flat, waiting for you.'

Flora felt sick. Jennifer Caird here? It was proof, as if she didn't already know it, that Duncan had been lying to her. 'What can I do?' Duncan was saying.

'Can't you tell her you're at that Reform Club thing?'

'It's her birthday, sweet. She can get frightfully prickly about that kind of stuff.'

Flora turned away from the tape. She couldn't bear to look at it.

'A late sitting, then?' Jennifer said. 'She'll never know. Two minutes, Duncan. You could be here.'

'Did you find it? My pressie? I left it on the sidetable. Gift-wrapped.'

'Oh, that,' Jennifer said. 'You mean the black lace number with the slit in the crotch? It just so happens I'm wearing it, my darling.'

'So where are you?'

'On your bed.'

Flora looked towards the bedroom and closed her eyes, overwhelmed by a feeling of nausea.

'Can you smell me on it? From last night?'

'Yes, yes, I can smell you,' Jennifer said softly. 'Acrid? Dark? Sweet like honey? Yes, sweet like honey.'

A moan of rage and pain exploded in Flora's head. She hurled herself into the bedroom and stripped off the duvet.

She could still hear the tape from the sitting-room.

'Turn over and spread yourself, lovely. I'm on my way.'

Flora, sobbing, snatched up the sheet, pulling and rending it.

'Really?'

'I'll phone her, make some excuse.'

'Jesus, I'm wet, Duncan . . . I'm soaking. How the hell do you do that to me?'

Flora was gulping, choking on her tears, and tugging at the sheet, again and again, with hysterical strength. The sheet split and tore into shards. The tape halted, and she sank onto the dishevelled bed, wracked by anguish and rage. She lay on the bed for a few moments, gasping for breath. Gradually, she became calmer. She opened her eyes, and the first thing she saw was the telephone diary, attached to the bedside phone. Sliding over the bed, she tugged out the diary and skimmed down the list of pre-set numbers, all named. There was the Whitehall office, Duncan's researcher, Central Office, a few restaurants, Flora, Ian Ruby-Smith. Only one number, T8, had a blank next to it. Flora reached out a forefinger and touched T8 on the pre-set buttons.

'This is Jennifer Caird's answerphone,' responded the all-too-familiar voice. 'Sorry I can't take your call at the moment, but if you'd –' Flora disconnected abruptly.

She got up and went into the sitting-room, looking for another bottle of wine. But her eyes kept going to the photographs and tapes. Scooping them up, she pushed them into her overnight case. The television was still on and Flora could see Duncan smiling confidently at her from the *Newsnight* studio. She didn't bother to turn up the sound.

Again she felt that pull towards the red boxes. Crossing the room, she rested a hand on them, and then gazed out of the window.

When was it she had promised to do that television interview? Some time later this week? She couldn't remember. But she could remember Alison Sissons, the girl from *Face the Famous*, on the answering machine . . . 'Anything we can do, you've got our number.'

There was a dawning, speculative look in Flora's eyes as she looked out of the window at the luminous spires of Parliament, like someone weighing up their adversary.

10

'Flora Matlock for the Jonathan Gilbert interview,' called out the receptionist at the Television Centre.

Flora stood up. 'That's me.'

'Surely not,' said Duncan, who had come to keep an eye on Flora's interview. 'Not Jonathan Gilbert?'

'Why not?' said Flora.

Mark, standing beside them, observed that Flora was remarkably calm for somebody who was not a television regular. He was also conscious that there was no glint in her eye, no acknowledgement of his visit the other evening.

'Because he only interviews royalty and prime ministers and so on,' said Duncan. 'Not ordinary people.'

'I'm not ordinary,' Flora said with a smile, 'I'm married to you.'

Duncan nodded. 'Well, it's a terrific honour he's chosen you, for whatever reason.'

'He didn't choose me,' Flora said, 'I asked him if he'd do the interview. I knew Central Office wanted me to do a television interview of one sort or another and I wanted the best.'

'Great.' Duncan was somewhat surprised at her incisiveness.

Flora headed towards the reception desk. 'I'm Flora Matlock. The Jonathan Gilbert interview.'

The receptionist pointed to the lifts. 'Fourth floor. Phil Spencer, Mr Gilbert's director, will be waiting for you. Oh, I'm sorry, sir.' She raised a restraining hand as Duncan started to follow Flora to the lift. 'I'm afraid I have only the one pass, for Mrs Matlock.'

'I think you may have made a mistake there,' Duncan said. 'My name is Duncan Matlock. I had a clear understanding that I would be present in the studio during my wife's interview.'

'No, I'm sorry, sir,' said the receptionist. 'Mr Gilbert never allows anyone into the studio when he is conducting an interview.' She smiled and helpfully indicated the leather benches beside an array of television screens. 'But you can stay here and watch it if you like.'

Duncan suppressed a flash of anger. He squeezed Flora's arm: 'Good luck, my love.'

Flora smiled at him as the lift doors closed.

'Hullo, Mrs Matlock,' Phil said, as she arrived at the fourth floor. 'It's good to see you again.'

'Good to see you, too,' said Flora. 'I hope this is a promotion from *Face the Famous*.'

'I'll say. Listen, I'm really sorry about all this business. So are Alison and Donnie – they send their good wishes, by the way.'

'Thank you,' said Flora. 'You've all been very helpful.'

Leading the way along a seemingly never-ending corridor, Phil said, 'We'll go to the office first, if that's okay with you. I told Jonathan that you were prepared to be absolutely up-front and I know he's got one of two ideas he'd like to talk through with you.'

'Hold on,' said Duncan. He was already displeased, having sat in reception for three-quarters of an hour, drinking disgusting coffee out of cardboard cups; and now he was being faced by six identical images of his wife speaking frankly about his private life. 'Wasn't that last question dangerously near the bone?'

'In the best possible taste,' said Mark.

'So how did you find out about the affair?' Jonathan was saying.

'From my husband,' Flora replied simply.

'And can you recall how you felt?'

'Disbelief. Initially, anyway.'

The panoply of screens showed Flora's face in close-up. The painful memory of it seemed momentarily to overtake her, but she swiftly composed herself.

'For God's sake,' Duncan turned on Mark: 'I thought the questions were vetted?'

'I understood she was going to vet them herself,' Mark replied. 'Before the programme.'

'And why do you suppose it always seems to be Conservative Ministers who are at the centre of these sexual scandals?' Jonathan smiled at Flora encouragingly.

'I know people think it's to do with background . . . the cloistered claustrophobia of public schools and all that.' Flora appeared to be thinking it through as she went along. 'But I believe it's something else. Perhaps the sheer responsibility of running the country puts such an untenable pressure on a man that he sometimes feels the need to seek physical release . . . without emotion or responsibility . . .' There was another close-up as she broke off, as if this line of thought was too distressing to pursue.

Mark flashed Duncan a look. His face was a study in confusion – he was not sure where all this was leading.

'And what do you say to the criticism that you, and politicians' wives like you, who stand by your errant husbands, are colluding in their hypocrisy?' Jonathan said.

'Politicians have had peccadilloes since Lloyd George's day, haven't they?' Flora replied.

Duncan, relaxed a little and nodded approvingly. 'That's good.'

'The Welsh goat, I believe he was called?' Jonathan said, grinning.

'Oh, really?' Flora smiled politely, as if the remark was mildly distasteful. 'They never made the headlines in those days, did they? But, since the Opposition has been ineffective for so long, the Press feels free to step in and morally chastise Ministers for their occasional sexual indiscretions ... knowing that it sells their newspapers. So who's the hypocrite there?'

'Bloody breathtaking, isn't she?' Duncan said, now totally relaxed.

'Indeed, yes,' said Mark.

'And the future, Mrs Matlock? Your thoughts on that?'

'When something like this happens you look to see if in some way you were to blame. At least, that's what I did.' The cameras closed in on Flora again, serenely confident. 'The conclusion I came to is that I must try and share my husband's work more. I mean the front-line Parliamentary stuff. If I can share that burden with him, then perhaps I can share some of the pressures, too.'

'I'm really proud of you, darling, you know that?' Duncan said. They were in the flat, changing for dinner, and Flora was basking in his approbation. 'I was a bit worried at the beginning, but you really pulled it your way.'

'I only said what I felt,' said Flora, zipping up the back of her all-occasions little black dress.

'Oh, how about the midnight-blue velvet, the thing you wore the other night?' Duncan said. 'I may not have mentioned it at the time, but you looked fantastic in that. Bloody radiant. No one could keep their eyes off you.'

'Everyone would be looking at me, no matter what I was wearing,' Flora said wryly. 'Anyway, it's a bit over-the-top for the House of Commons restaurant, wouldn't you say?'

'Right as usual, my love.' Duncan planted a kiss on top of her head. 'Come on, sweetheart, or we'll be late for your party.'

Flora and Duncan were the last to arrive. The restaurant was full of MPs and their guests, but they found Sir Donald, Mark Hollister, Ian Ruby-Smith and Clive Woodley already seated around a large circular table in the centre of the room.

'Table of honour for the guest of honour.' Sir Donald stood and kissed Flora. 'Come and sit here, next to me and your father. Magnificent performance, my dear,' he murmured as they sat down.

'Well, Flo,' Clive said, 'you certainly surprised me. They'll be giving you your own programme next.' He gave Flora's hand an affectionate pat. 'This calls for a celebration.'

'Absolutely right, Clive,' said Sir Donald. 'A bottle of the Widow, would you say?' He called over the waiter and ordered the Veuve Clicquot.

'Excuse me.' A young man appeared at Flora's elbow as she was preparing to tackle her hors-d'œuvre. 'I just wanted to say bravo,' he said breathlessly. 'Really. Everyone at Central Office thought it an absolute wow.'

'I only said what I felt,' Flora repeated, putting down her knife and fork and smiling at the young man.

'Which is just why it rang so true,' he said, blushing. 'Well done.' He nodded to the others around the table and retreated swiftly.

A number of people, who had followed this little tableau, were now staring at Flora, some with frank curiosity, others in covert sympathy. Flora knew she should be getting used to this, but was unable to conceal a quiver of humiliation.

Sir Donald, recognising her expression and its cause, raised his glass. 'In my capacity as chief cheerleader . . . to Flora.'

They all lifted their glasses. 'To Flora.' Clive kissed her cheek.

Two couples at a nearby table echoed this with a ripple of courteous applause. Flora lowered her eyes in embarrassment. When she looked up, it was straight into the eyes of Mark Hollister.

'Any word from the PM yet?' Clive asked Sir Donald.

'He's much relieved,' Sir Donald said. 'The last thing we need right now is another political death by slow torture. Mind you, as he pointed out, we have the second phase to ride out yet. When the quality leaders weigh in.'

'You anticipate a problem there, then?' Clive asked.

'We can assume the Ministry for the Family will be subjected to the full rigour of their myopic scrutiny,' Sir Donald replied. He nodded at Duncan. 'Those that get a whiff of your Bill will be the most irksome.'

Flora, who had been following the minutiae of all this, glanced at him quickly. 'Is it going to be that controversial?'

Sir Donald swiftly deflected the question by holding up his fork, pronged with a piece of meat. 'What's in this?' he asked, smiling at Flora. 'Coriander?'

'Cumin,' said Flora.

'With lamb?' said Sir Donald. 'Are they mad? What became of good old fashioned garlic and rosemary?'

Flora merely smiled at him, well aware that she was being side-tracked.

'The back-bench Chinese whispers are already on overdrive,' Ian said to Duncan. 'A bad press might just start a stampede.'

Flora was intrigued. What, she wondered, was so controversial about this Bill to have them all so worried?

'Unless you use the well-tried wolf-wolf tactic,' said Sir Donald.

'Wolf-what tactic?' Flora was looking from one to the other. Mark Hollister was watching her.

'You let everyone think the piece of impending legislation is actually far worse than it is . . .' Mark said.

'So, when you finally go public,' Duncan concluded, 'it's greeted by sighs of relief all round.'

Flora raised an eyebrow. 'How ingenious.' She scanned the menu eagerly. It was the first time for days she had fancied food and she was ravenous.

'It has the added advantage of discrediting your critics as alarmists and bullshitters,' Ian said.

'Doubly ingenious,' said Flora. My God, she was thinking, was that all politics meant to them? Strategies and mendacity?

Mark, who had been glancing around the room, suddenly sat bolt upright. 'Dear God. Is this some kind of joke?'

Everyone followed his gaze to the doorway, where Jennifer Caird was entering on the arm of an elderly MP.

Shit! thought Duncan, and just when everything was shaping up so nicely. 'Grace under pressure, chaps,' he said. 'Let's not turn a squall into a storm.'

The couple were shown to a table at the other side of the room. There was a ripple of curiosity around the restaurant and eyes flicked eagerly from Jennifer Caird to Flora.

'Isn't that Binkie Alsop with her?' said Sir Donald. He scrutinised Duncan's mistress with interest and decided that she'd got far too much stuff slapped on her face – the make-up people must have taken it off for that breakfast programme instead of putting it on. The thought amused him.

'As large as bloody life,' said Ian, wondering why Sir Donald was smirking. He could hardly wait to get home and tell his wife about this latest scene in the drama.

Sir Donald shook his head in amazement. 'Has his IQ gone completely AWOL?'

Ian smiled. 'It was a meagre thing at best.'

Grinning around the table, Duncan said: 'If it got any lower, you'd have to water it.'

Everybody laughed at this, except Flora. She couldn't believe that their interest was focused on an old man with a foolish name, rather than on her feelings. She wished she'd worn the blue velvet, the red, anything other than this boring, dowdy black dress from County Classics of Carlingham. Jennifer was wearing a well-cut cream silk trouser-suit. Armani was Flora's guess. She looked away, as an image flashed into her mind of Jennifer Caird, rather more informally dressed in Duncan's present. Pressie! How she despised that word.

She shuddered slightly, and Duncan, over the other side of the table, sensed her unease. 'Just say the word, darling. We can dodge out any time you want.'

'Gracious, no,' Flora said. 'I want to see the dessert trolley.'

She was just finishing her profiteroles when she noticed Jennifer Caird leaving her table and heading for an exit. Flora waited a few minutes and got up from the table. 'If you'll all excuse me.'

'Of course.' The men half-rose, clutching their napkins. A group of gentlemen.

Flora found herself in a vaulted corridor with stained-glass windows. On the way to the stairs, she passed two men she assumed to be MPs. They looked at her curiously and she overheard one say to the other: 'Isn't that Matlock's wife, the one who . . . ?'

Flora quickened her step, up the stairs and into the room discreetly labelled Ladies. The panelled room was more like a library than a lavatory. Flora looked around. There were three cubicles and only one was occupied. Flora locked the outer door and positioned herself across the room from the hand-basins.

Jennifer Caird stepped out and, seeing Flora, halted momentarily. Clearly she was making a determined effort not to appear disconcerted. She strolled over to one of the hand-basins and turned on the tap. 'Bit of a dump, isn't it?' she said casually. 'You'd have thought Maggie would have made the female bogs a priority.'

Flora, standing in the shadow of the vaulted doorway, did not reply. Someone rattled the outer door handle and Jennifer looked up, a flicker of apprehension in her face. Then, ignoring Flora, she sat down at the mirror and took out her make-up bag.

'I'd like your view on something,' Flora said.

Jennifer pursed her lips, applied some lipstick, and waited. She could see Flora's reflection in the mirror.

'I'm wondering,' – Flora's voice was coldly dispassionate – 'whether you go along with the theory that what separates human beings from animals is that we have a conscience?'

Jennifer allowed herself an amused glance in the mirror while she collected her thoughts. 'You could put it another way,' she said. 'You could say that what separates us from the animals is that they don't deny their primal urges.'

The gibe found its target. Flora had a swift picture of Jennifer Caird on breakfast television, legs demurely tucked under her chair, and heard again the hurtful words, 'particularly if their wives are passive or sexually unadventurous . . .'

'Maybe a conscience is primal, too,' she said. 'Maybe it's genetic. You're either born with it or without it.'

Jennifer smiled and said nothing. She seemed in control of the situation, but Flora noticed a tremor in her hands as she pushed the cosmetics back into the make-up bag.

'Well', Flora unlocked the door. 'Perhaps one day they'll isolate the gene. Then we'll be equal.'

She was gone before Jennifer could reply. Jennifer stared at her reflection in the mirror. Of course I've got a conscience, she said to herself. I'd never even met his bloody wife when I got into bed with him, had I? And then it was too late. Seeing her . . . well, it was odd, somehow. She didn't fit the role of Duncan's passive sister, the Wife Who Doesn't Do It. Actually, she was rather attractive. Jennifer tossed back her long hair and licked her lips in readiness for her second entrance. Men! she thought. Bloody liars, the lot of them.

Flora and Mark left the restaurant together. The others were some way behind, having been waylaid by a backbencher anxious to discuss a constituency problem with Sir Donald and Duncan.

'The other evening . . .' Mark looked questioningly at Flora. 'Have you given the matter any thought?'

'I've thought of nothing else,' Flora said.

'And . . . ?'

It was a moment before Flora answered. 'When I was a child, I thought Jesus was always behind me, watching out for me, if you see what I mean. I used to whip round, hoping to see him. Once I imagined I'd caught a glimpse of his white robe darting behind a tree.' She paused to acknowledge a security guard in the lobby. 'Or perhaps it was just Satan.'

'Or a friend, trying to help,' Mark said softly.

Flora turned and looked at him. 'Help himself, or me?'

'Hang on, you two,' Duncan called out. 'We're having a very constructive discussion here . . .'

'About where we're going to go now,' said Sir Donald. 'It seems a pity to break up such a pleasant evening.'

They strolled out through St Stephen's Gate and Duncan signalled to his waiting car.

'Do you want to go on somewhere?' Flora asked him.

'Are you up to it?' Duncan was obviously raring to go.

'Not me,' said Flora. 'Heavens, I can barely put one foot in front of the other. That doesn't have to stop you, though.'

'How about the Griffin?' said Clive, enjoying this moment close to the seat of power.

'A morgue, this time of night,' said Sir Donald. 'The Carlton?'

'Sounds good to me,' said Duncan.

'I'll bow out,' said Mark. 'Things to do. Nice to see you again, Flora.'

'You too, Mark,' Flora said.

Sir Donald put an arm around Flora's shoulders. 'We should talk, my dear. One or two loose ends need tying.'

'Whatever you say.' Flora smiled at him and kissed his cheek.

They all hovered attentively as Flora got into the car and it glided off.

'Well, she certainly came through,' said Sir Donald.

'One hundred per cent,' said Clive. 'That's my girl.'

'One hundred and one, I'd say,' said Ian.

Duncan, speaking to the group but looking at Sir Donald, said: 'Did you ever doubt it?'

'You get so used to observing the baser instincts in this place,' Sir Donald remarked, 'that you tend to forget there is any other kind of instinct.'

Flora was getting into bed when the phone rang. It was Paul, wanting to know when she was coming home.

'Tomorrow night, darling,' she said. 'Wednesday at the latest.'

She did not miss the edge to his voice when he said, 'Is he coming back, too?'

'At the weekend, pet. How's Joanna?'

'In bed,' said Paul. 'Asleep.'

'Where you should be,' said his mother.

'Can't sleep.'

'All right.' Flora settled down in bed, the phone to her ear. 'Talk to me.'

'Mrs Lucas dished up another of her yucky shepherd's pies tonight,' said Paul. 'And the starlings are back. Hundreds of them. They turned the sky really black.'

Flora was overwhelmed by the memory of Mindermere, of all that was safe and familiar. 'You're the best, Paul,' she said.

'You're the second best,' Paul replied.

'Bed, okay?'

'Mum . . . ?'

'Yes, darling?'

'I love you.'

'And I you, my darling,' Flora said. There were tears in her eyes as she put down the phone.

Flora was not asleep when Duncan returned, but she pretended to be. She could hear him tugging off his clothes and then he was crawling in and snuggling up behind her.

'Flora?' His hand moved caressingly down her body. He felt a heartfelt love for her, an indebtedness which was stronger than love itself.

Flora stifled a spasm of repugnance, but her voice **was** tender as she whispered: 'I can't, my sweet. My period.'

Duncan removed his hand. 'It's gone on since for ever.'

Flora yawned. 'It's the stress, I expect,' she said.

11

Flora had been home at Mindermere for a couple of days when Charlotte rang and suggested lunch. 'I did call you back when . . . well, you know . . .' Charlotte said. 'Left a message on the answering machine.'

Flora remembered the need she'd felt to drown Charlotte's voice with the lavatory flush, but she decided to be charitable. Maybe she would have rushed to the phone with equally ill-concealed excitement if it had been Charlotte's husband's sex-life plastered all over the morning papers. 'So many messages,' she said vaguely. 'But I have got a few people to see in London next week.'

'Good,' said Charlotte. 'How about Tuesday, one o'clock, Harvey Nichols fifth-floor café? Café not restaurant, right?'

'Right,' said Flora.

'Just beyond the astonishingly pricey groceries. You can't book at lunch so I'll get there early and grab a table.'

Rounding Belgrave Square, Flora looked at her watch. Twelve-thirty. She'd left Mindermere House just after 9.30. Congratulating herself on her timing, she swung round the corner and drove down into the Harvey Nichols car-park.

Charlotte was sitting in the window of the café, sipping a glass of white wine. There was a bottle on the table in front of her. 'Flora!'

Flora leant forward, about to brush Charlotte's cheek with hers, but Charlotte jumped up and hugged her. 'Oh, Flora, you look bloody marvellous, do you know that?'

'I don't feel particularly marvellous,' Flora said. 'I've just driven up from Mindermere –'

'Oh dear.' Charlotte looked sympathetic and poured Flora a glass of wine. 'Reporters, cameras, all that?'

'Not now, no.' Flora raised her glass and smiled at Charlotte; she was really pleased to see her. 'No, that's all over. Except there's one reporter, a local stringer, I think, who's been camping at the end of the drive ever since the story broke.'

'Poor lamb.'

'Mrs Lucas takes him out cups of coffee and the children wave to him on their way to and from school,' Flora said. 'No, it's not the Press any more. It's the letters that are beginning to get to me.'

There had been piles of them waiting on the hall table when she'd got back from London. It had been so wonderful to be home. To hear that Joanna was going to be in the school play and had been chosen for the netball team. To say, 'Yes, of course it's all right,' when Paul asked if he could bring a friend home to tea. To see the magnolia bursting into blossom outside the dining-room window. And then the letters had spoilt it all. Of course there were some commiserating, some congratulating, some offering help. But there was hatred, too. What, they all wanted to know, had happened to her self-esteem and her self-respect? She was a stupid doormat who'd let any man wipe his filthy feet on her; she was a disgrace to womankind and she was letting down her sisters. Worse, she was aiding and abetting an adulterer. 'He should be punished,' wrote one correspondent. 'He hasn't been punished enough.'

Soon she learnt to leave the envelopes with mad, erratic writing unopened until she was sitting comfortably, next to a stiff drink. But even the neatly typed ones leaked occasional bile.

'There's such a lack of compassion,' she told Charlotte later, as she spooned pesto sauce over her chicken. 'Do you know what I was called today?'

'How about "a remarkably resilient woman"?' said Charlotte.

'Try "power groupie",' said Flora. 'I've ruthlessly propelled my man to the top and now I'm hanging on in there for the political power and glory. Several of them have said that.'

'What nonsense,' Charlotte said briskly. 'You got a two-one, a better degree than he did. I know, because I was there . . . you didn't need to group round anyone. You were always too good for him, Flora.'

'Duncan would have got a first if he hadn't done so many other things. The debating, the rowing, the rugby, all that,' Flora replied, automatically loyal, and then gazed throughtfully into her house white. 'It's funny, you know, I always had the impression that everyone at Cambridge thought he was too good for me.'

'Huh,' Charlotte said, 'I expect he told you that. And you'd have got a first if you hadn't been hanging around doing his laundry and cooking cosy little suppers for him, all *that*.' Charlotte, a corporate lawyer, had never fixed a cosy little supper for anyone. She was married to a venture capitalist who took them both out to dinner on the days when he hadn't managed to fix up a business lunch. She had often wondered why her friend had chosen to subjugate her life to Duncan Matlock's political career. 'And are they right about the power and glory? Is that why you haven't dumped him?'

'I love Duncan,' said Flora. 'I believed him when he said that what he was doing was important, both for the party and the country.' She grinned as Charlotte raised a cynical eyebrow. 'No, honestly. But as for the power and the glory –

do we mean chatting up the Lord Mayor? Or sitting on local committees discussing traffic movements? Or has it to do with stuffing 500 photographs of one's husband into envelopes? This is strictly second-hand power.'

'I'd go for revenge, if it was me,' Charlotte said. 'Like that Moon woman. You know, cutting off the sleeves of the Savile Row suits, delivering cases of his best vintage wines to everyone in the village.'

'Not very subtle, is it?'

'Well, then, how about stuffing the curtain rail with bad prawns?' Charlotte refilled their glasses. 'That's really my favourite. No, useless, come to think of it, unless you're moving out or he's leaving with the curtains and fixtures. I know.' She called for the bill. 'Have you got half an hour? Armani, just down the road, there's a cream silk trouser-suit in the window. Do you a treat.'

Back at the flat, Flora took the trouser-suit out of the Emporio Armani bag and hung it up in the wardrobe, next to Duncan's spare London pin-stripe. Much too expensive, but she'd been carried away by Charlotte's enthusiasm, and by the notion, lurking somewhere at the back of her mind, that a cream silk Armani trouser-suit would automatically transform her into a sophisticated, desirable woman. 'And you'd better have that silk camisole top, too,' Charlotte had said, 'or you'll be revealing far too much to the Lord Mayor.'

Slipping into the camisole, Flora had said: 'She isn't a bimbo, you know.'

'Who?' Charlotte looked at Flora's face. 'Oh, her. So you *did* get my message. Sarah and I had been celebrating. That's why –'

'It's all right now,' Flora had reassured her. 'Really. It's just that nobody seems to realise, when they criticise the

Other Woman, that it's even more humiliating if your husband is besotted with someone absolutely ghastly.'

'And she's not? I mean, escort agencies and all that?'

'No,' Flora had replied, appraising herself in the mirror. 'Actually, she's attractive, quite formidably so.'

And now she sat at Duncan's desk, considering with pleasure how she was about to curtail Jennifer Caird's activities. But first she had something else to do.

She lifted Duncan's box files from the shelf above the desk and sorted through the contents. Swiftly separating the ones she needed, she put them in the fax copier. When the papers were copied, she replaced the originals in the box files. As she was putting away the files, she came across something – a duster, maybe? – at the back of the shelf. She pulled it out. It was nothing so wholesome as a duster. Flora felt a flash of outrage as she realised she was holding Duncan's present, the black lace item with a hole in the crotch. She slid a finger experimentally through the hole and then, fastidiously, with forefinger and thumb, dropped the underwear in her bag. Speedily clipping the papers together, she put them into her handbag, too.

There was a book on the desk marked 'Register of Members' Interests.' Flora picked it up and, leafing idly through it, came to the entry. 'MATLOCK, DUNCAN (Carlingham).' Underneath it read: 'Financial Sponsorships, Gifts, etc – Nil. Directorships – Director, Marlborough Insurance (to 19.7.81).' Flora made a note of this. She had an instinct that, one day, this information just might come in useful.

Flora felt good the following morning. She'd had a long talk with the children on the phone, followed by two slices of toasted cheese in front of the television and an early night. Duncan hadn't returned home until nearly one a.m. Sir Donald had taken him off to his dining club, to brief a group of influential Parliamentarians about his upcoming Bill. In the morning he'd jumped out of bed and kissed her briefly ('Bye, sweet. Going shopping? Have fun') and had dashed off for a breakfast meeting with the Secretary of State for Social Security. 'Late sitting in the House tonight,' he'd called out from the front door. 'See you Friday, anyway. Take care.'

And now, Flora was signing in at the high-tech glass security desk of the Ministry for the Family in Whitehall. She had another lunch date.

The officer checked her MP's Wife Pass and said: 'You're here to see – ?'

'Lydia Gibb, my husband's researcher,' said Flora. She passed through the two sets of glass security doors with practised ease and went towards the lifts and the cafeteria.

Lydia was already queuing at the self-service counter. She was in her early thirties, chubby and tirelessly efficient. And, with her glasses hanging on a string around her neck, she looked, Flora noted with amusement, more like a staff nurse than the kind of sexually voracious parliamentary researcher Charlotte had warned her about so long ago.

Flora joined Lydia as she piled her plate with meat pasties, baked beans and chips. 'Like school dinners, isn't it?' Lydia said. 'They tried a *cordon bleu* menu but the chaps got up a three-line whip. Couldn't bear the idea of losing their stodge.' Flora smiled politely, all too aware that the MPs, researchers and parliamentary workers lunching at the Formica tables were studying her with unabashed interest. Lydia, equally aware, threw Flora a glance of compassion. 'Was it awfully rough?' she said, as they unloaded their trays at a vacant table.

'Pretty dire,' Flora said.

'I just can't believe he was such a prat,' Lydia said vehemently. 'Half of them in this room are at it, you know.

That's why it gets to them. There but for the grace of God, et cetera.' Flora nodded. 'See that man over there . . .' Flora followed Lydia's gaze to where a nondescript-looking grey-haired man in a dreary grey suit was morosely eating fish and chips. 'Six months ago, his wife found out he'd been having an affair with his secretary,' said Lydia. 'She keeps tabs on him with his mobile phone. He has to ring her throughout the day to say where he is and who he's with, and if he's invited to a function she hot-foots it up from the country to be by his side.'

'Sounds exhausting,' Flora said.

There was an awkward pause. They both concentrated on their food. Eventually, Lydia said: 'she's still around, you know.'

'Yes, I know.'

'What I don't understand is how on earth she talked anyone into giving her a research post? Only a crusty old fart like Naylor would fall for it. He hasn't spoken in the House since the year dot.' Lydia waved her fork around the room. 'The gays like them, though, the ones the whips haven't succeeded in marrying off. Her sort act as chaperones, stop the tongues wagging. That's what they really mean by escort girls.'

Flora shook her head in amazement, taking it all in.

'It's so bloody demeaning. Not just for Commons researchers. For the party. For all of us.'

'Yes, I know,' Flora said.

Lydia, instantly contrite, clapped a hand to her mouth. 'Duncan always says I've got the tact of a Sumo wrestler.'

'He also says you're the best researcher in the City of Westminster,' said Flora.

Lydia grinned ruefully. 'He should try saying it to my face sometimes.'

Flora put down her knife and fork and leaned forward

confidentially. 'It was my fault, Lydia,' she said seriously, 'All of it.' Lydia, startled, stared at her. 'I haven't helped Duncan enough. I should be part of his life here, share it with him, support him.' Lydia looked at Flora questioningly. 'If he's going out on a limb on this Bill, I want to be out there with him; every inch of the way. Not sitting at home and hearing about it second-hand from Jeremy Paxman.'

Touched and impressed by Flora's sincerity, Lydia took her hand and squeezed it. 'Is there anything I can do?'

'I need a favour.' Flora smiled sweetly. 'And I need it to be just between us two.'

After lunching with Lydia, Flora had been to Harrods to stock up on Paul's school uniform. Now she was sitting in the back of a taxi outside the House of Commons, watching MPs, parlimentary workers and visitors drift out of St Stephen's Gate. Eventually, she spotted Gordon Naylor. He was leaning on a stick, looking around vaguely for a taxi.

'Two minutes,' Flora said to her driver. She jumped out of the taxi and went over to the elderly MP. 'Mr Naylor?' He squinted at her blankly. 'Flora Matlock. I wondered if I could have a word?' She slid her arm through his and guided him to her parked taxi.

Gordon Naylor was confused. Pretty woman . . . familiar name. 'What?'

'Sorry to hijack you like this.' Flora helped him into the taxi. 'But every time I turn round these days the paparazzi jump out at me. It's about Jennifer Caird.'

Jennifer Caird. Gordon Naylor made the connection with Flora Matlock and said apologetically, 'Ghastly business. I don't have to tell you . . .'

His voice trailed off and Flora said: 'This really is *so* embarrassing.'

Gordon Naylor blinked at her, hoping it was not going to be as embarrassing as he suspected.

'The other night,' Flora said, 'In the House restaurant. She was there.'

'Oh, Lord.'

'The fact that she was there at all suggests that she still has her security pass.'

'She shouldn't have.' Gordon Naylor felt on firmer ground. 'I dispensed with her services the moment the story –'

'These bureaucratic blips can be so tiresome, can't they?' Flora said sympathetically. 'Perhaps if you could speak to the Sergeant at Arms – expedite things?'

'Consider it done.' Gordon Naylor made a move to leave the taxi and Flora put out a restraining hand.

'Mr Naylor?' He swivelled, gloomily. 'I know you're a man of influence.' She smiled at him admiringly. 'How about The Footstool Restaurant? Rodins? L'Amico's? My husband and I dine at all of them quite often.'

'Leave it to me, my dear.' He nodded at her in embarrassed acknowledgement.

'I'm so grateful, Mr Naylor,' Flora said as the old man clambered thankfully out of the taxi. She leant back and watched him make his get-away as fast as his gout allowed him, and then she tugged her mobile phone out of her bag.

'Is he there?' she said crisply. Her voice became soft and compliant as she said: 'Hello, there. No, no. It's just that I'm due to go back to Mindermere tonight. I thought perhaps we could meet before I go? Over a drink at the flat? Fine, I'll look forward to it.' She hung up.

The driver looked at her through his mirror: 'Okay, lady. Where to now?'

'Mount Street,' Flora said. 'Nicky Clarke.'

*

There were pictures of Fergie in the loo at Nicky Clarke's, and on the wall facing the backwash. Wild-haired, jolly, out of control in the Before pictures; trimmed, slimmed and tamed down in the Afters. Flora lay back in the chair with her hair in the basin and decided she preferred Fergie Before. She hoped the £160-plus she was about to pay for her own transformation was not going straight down the drain.

The highlights did, in the event, change her dramatically from a dull, brown, country mouse sort of person into something rather exotic. And the cut, which needed three people to achieve (one assistant passing scissors and pins, one holding up the hair, one stylist cutting it) was shorter, bouncier and more youthful. Or, as the girl in reception said: 'Amazing, Mrs Matlock. You look *years* younger than when you came in.' This made Flora depressed about how old she must have looked at half-past three. The reception was kitted out like a country house with a mock log fire and deep armchairs and she was tempted to opt out of the next few hours, settle down and browse through the magazines.

She didn't, of course. She took a taxi through the evening rush-hour traffic, and looking at the meter, decided that she had possibly spent the most expensive two days of her life. Back in the flat, conscious of the fact that steam would undo the hair, Flora had a lukewarm bath. Lying there, soaking in Floris's Stephanotis, she realised that the weeks of misery, anger and humiliation had caused her to lose at least a stone in weight. So she had paid an even higher price for the figure than for the hairstyle and taxis.

She did her face and then put on the new Armani, surveying herself in the mirror. She seemed to be spending an awful lot of time looking in mirrors these days. And what she saw was not totally pleasing. She certainly looked different. And the cream silk trouser-suit did, as Charlotte had predicted, do her a treat. But she felt somehow disconcerted by this elegant sylph in the mirror ... diminished. She looked like somebody else.

She wrenched off the jacket, slung it on the bed and was just about to unzip the trousers when she remembered the tape in her overnight bag. She took it out and considered it. Why did she keep torturing herself with these tapes? It was like the compulsion to press on a sore tooth, to remind herself of the pain. She sighed and slipped the tape into the stereo cassette. The familiar voices of her husband and his mistress permeated the flat as she set a wine-bucket, a bottle of wine and two glasses on the coffee-table.

'Where is she now?' Jennifer said.

'On a duty call at her father's, with the kids,' Duncan replied.

'So when can you leave?'

'In an hour, lovely. Traffic allowing. I should be at your flat by eight.'

'Oh, my darling. I'll make it worth it, I promise you.'

'You will? How?'

'Wait and see.'

'Come on. Tell me . . .'

Flora, banging out the ice, wondered if she could possibly bear to hear another description of the curious postures Jennifer Caird adopted to greet her husband. She turned on the tap and rinsed out the two glasses, as Jennifer said huskily: 'Okay. This is how it will be. You'll let yourself in with your key. It'll be dark. Very dark. Dark as dark can be. At first you don't see anything. Then you put on the hall light. And I'm there crouched, squatting on the floor, waiting for you. You pretend to be shocked. Angry, to find me so wanton and –'

'Oh, for God's sake,' Flora said aloud as she put the glasses on the table.

She was just about to go back into the kitchen to collect

the wine when she heard Duncan's voice on the tape again. 'Shit! She's back.'

'Flora?'

'Yes, she's . . . hang on . . .' He called out: 'I'm on the phone, love.'

Flora went into the bedroom instead of the kitchen, put on the jacket and buttoned it grimly. She had thought she was becoming inured to these conversations, but the disloyalty of this last bit really got to her.

'It's okay,' Duncan was saying. 'She forgot something. She's gone.'

'That was a bit close for comfort, Duncan . . .'

Flora snapped off the stereo, her resolve strengthened, no longer doubtful or uncertain. Glancing through the window, she could see the spires of Parliament under a cloud-smeared evening sky. They, too, seemed to give her added strength.

The entry buzzer went. Flora pressed the front door release, gave the room a final check and then went into the hall. A second later there was a ring. Flora counted to three. Her face was wreathed in smiles as she opened the door to welcome Sir Donald Frazier.

'Am I late?' He lumbered in, dishevelled as ever, diminishing the tiny flat by his sheer presence.

'Punctual to the second,' Flora said. 'Just us, I'm afraid. Duncan's still at the House.'

Sir Donald looked around the room, noticed the wine, observed Flora's transformation, and felt a vague disquiet. 'You've done something to your hair.'

'I treated myself,' Flora said. 'Do you like it?'

Sir Donald. who was not in the habit of paying women compliments, said gruffly, 'Yes, indeed.'

Flora passed him a glass of wine as he sat down and opened his briefcase. 'Well, to business, my dear.' Taking out some papers, he handed them to Flora. 'Your latest press hit-list. My office drew it up. Call them with the ones you approve and they'll set up a schedule for you.'

There was a slight hiatus as Flora sipped her wine and scanned the papers.

'So,' Sir Donald said heartily. 'It's back to Mindermere, is it?'

'Soon as I can make it,' Flora said.

'Tell me,' Sir Donald said. 'How well do you know Rosalind Clegg?'

Flora was puzzled by this question. 'Well, naturally, we've been on committees . . .'

Sir Donald nodded: 'Of course. I thought, perhaps, you could have a quiet word? Woman to woman. These blue-rinse moral crusaders have a habit of coming back at you when you least expect it. We must make sure she holds the course.'

'Leave it with me.' Flora allowed a small pause before she leaned forward. 'I'm so glad of this chance to talk to you, Sir Donald. There's something I've been wanting to say.'

'Oh?' Sir Donald sounded uncomfortable.

'I know all about Jennifer Caird. I've known all along. I mean, that it lasted nearly a year. And that it was Duncan who initiated it.' Sir Donald knew he'd been right to feel uneasy. He stared at Flora; for once, he was at a loss for words. 'You lied to me,' she said.

'But only to protect you,' he answered swiftly.

'It's a little late for that, I'm afraid.' Flora lowered her voice. 'I know I can confide in you, Sir Donald.' Sir Donald, bemused, nodded. 'The truth is, Duncan finds passion within marriage to be a law of diminishing returns. So he seeks it elsewhere. He has done for years.' She was astonished, and rather shocked, to find how easily the lies rolled off her tongue.

Sir Donald stared at her in amazement. How could his

informants have got it so wrong? 'My understanding was that Jennifer Caird was a one-off affair,' he said. 'Unprecedented.'

'He told you that, did he?' There were tears in Flora's voice as she said: 'I've tried to put my feelings on hold – to accept it. For the children's sake as much as . . . not always easy, as you can imagine. I tell myself it's a test of loyalty – not just to Duncan, but to the party.' She looked up at Sir Donald, who found it difficult to meet her eyes. 'I felt so badly about deceiving you, of all people. After all your sterling work.'

Sir Donald said gruffly: 'I suppose I should thank you for your candour.'

'Oh.' Flora seemed distressed. 'I've disappointed you. You think me weak and –'

'Not you, my dear, never.' Sir Donald gathered his papers and briefcase and rose to leave. Had he sounded, perhaps, a little too terse? The truth was that Flora's revelations had upset him more than he would have expected. He bowed in an oddly old-fashioned manner. 'Well, my dear, thank you for your hospitality.'

Flora stopped him in mid-flight. 'Sir Donald?'

'Yes?'

'All those rumours about your own marriage?'

Sir Donald stared at her. 'What?'

'Duncan told me there have been whispers for years,' Flora said. 'That your wife turns a blind eye. I just want you to know that I never believed a word of it.'

'It appears that Duncan has been rather more selective with the truth than I appreciated,' Sir Donald said crisply. He was angry as he stomped out. 'Goodnight to you, Flora.'

After Sir Donald had left, Flora picked up a glass of wine, took a sip, and then tapped the glass thoughtfully. She had initiated a chain of events. She was not quite sure, yet, where it would lead.

12

Flora had arrived back at Mindermere to the sound of the dawn chorus. Getting out of the car, she put down her case and just stood there for a moment, listening to the chattering of the starlings, refreshed by the comforting contours of her house and cheered to discover that the *acer* leaves had not, this year, withered in the wind as she'd feared.

On her way upstairs, she noticed that Joanna's door was open. Flora paused in the doorway, savouring the sight of her sleeping daughter. Next door, Paul was moving restlessly in his bunk-bed, and she went quietly into the room and stroked his face with her forefinger. On the pinboard above his head, among the paraphernalia of pictures of pop stars and footballers and typed lists of school fixtures, was a photo of Paul riding piggyback on Duncan. Paul beaming with delight and Duncan laughing, head thrown back, boyish and wind-blown. Flora remembered snapping that happy scene in the garden last summer. It felt like another life.

From her bedroom window, she looked out on a translucent morning mist hanging over the drive and gardens: it seemed to her like a veil of tears. She went over to the answering machine. The first call was from Richard Pearson, Paul's housemaster. 'If you could phone me,' he said, 'I'd be most grateful.'

Flora was apprehensive. Schoolmasters did not, in her experience, ring up parents mid-term to report satisfactory progress in the classroom or on the sports field. Flora had

105

reckoned that she could get in a few hours of sleep before seeing the children off to school, but nagged by anxiety she slept only fitfully. Eventually she decided she might just as well get up, go downstairs, and get herself a cup of coffee.

Mrs Lucas was already in the kitchen, feeding Basker and assembling cereals and toast for the children's breakfast. On sighting Flora, Basker went wild with pleasure, leaving his bowl of Chappie and prancing delightedly around her.

'Well, that's the first time I've seen Basker willingly leave a half-full bowl of food,' Mrs Lucas said. 'Not that I'm not pleased to see you back, as well, Mrs Matlock. And just wait until Joanna and Paul come down . . .'

Helping herself to coffee from the pot on the Aga, Flora looked over at Mrs Lucas. 'They've been all right?'

'Joanna – right as rain,' Mrs Lucas said. 'Very taken up with the play; we've all had to hear her lines.'

'And Paul?'

'Still a bit withdrawn. Mr Lucas has been teaching him to play chess these last few days.' Mrs Lucas grinned at Flora as she put fresh marmalade into the pot. 'Between ourselves, Mrs Matlock, Paul was beating him by the third game.'

'You're both very kind,' Flora said. 'I don't know what I'd do without you.' She stirred her coffee, thinking what a lucky day it had been when Mrs Lucas walked through the door. It was seven years ago. She'd come to Mindermere House as a cleaner and very soon it had become apparent that she was much better with Joanna and Paul than the army of au pair girls Flora had hired to help with the children. Gradually, Mrs Lucas had taken on more, stayed later, and had become the Matlocks' housekeeper. When Flora and Duncan were away from home, she and her husband Dave, the local milkman, moved into one of the spare rooms and became proxy parents. Flora often thought they did the job better than she or Duncan.

106

'I've got Mr Pearson, Paul's housemaster, on my answer-phone,' she said. 'Wants to speak to me. I suppose you don't have any idea – ?'

'Not a clue, I'm afraid, Mrs Matlock,' said Mrs Lucas. 'I just collect and deliver; I've hardly spoken to a soul.'

'I hope the school run hasn't been a problem?' Flora always worried that she was overloading Mrs Lucas with tasks.

'Not a bit of it,' said Mrs Lucas, 'but I think a lot of the mothers have been disappointed to see me getting out of the car instead of the famous politician's wife.'

'Not the kind of fame I'd wish on anyone,' Flora said.

'No, of course not,' Mrs Lucas said quickly. 'I didn't mean to speak out of turn. It's just that Mr Lucas and I did think you were very good on that television programme. Better than Anne Diamond or any of them, Mr Lucas said.'

'It seems so long ago,' Flora said. She'd almost forgotten Jonathan Gilbert.

'Well, I'd have mentioned it last time you were home, only you were so busy with all that post and everything. Paul was very keen to see it. He asked me to video it for him.'

'Oh dear.'

'Not to worry, Mrs Matlock.' Mrs Lucas poured them both another cup of coffee. 'You know how hopeless I am with machinery. I must have set it wrong.'

'Thank you, Mrs Lucas,' Flora said. She was smiling as she carried her coffee into Duncan's study to answer the phone.

'Are you ready for the fax?' Lydia Gibb called out cheerfully. 'I'm putting it through now.'

'Perfect timing.' Flora watched the paper coil across the desk and then spill onto the floor. The machine bleeped and she picked up the phone.

'Did you get it all?' Lydia asked.

'Fourteen pages?' said Flora.

'Okay. Call me if you need any more,' said Lydia.

Flora was just starting to check the fax when she heard noises in the hall. Going out to investigate, she found Mrs Lucas in her coat, car keys in hand, overseeing Joanna and Paul's departure for school.

'Mum!' Joanna hurled herself into her mother's arms.

Flora hugged her. 'Have you got everything, darling?' She turned to Mrs Lucas. 'Are you sure, Mrs Lucas? I can easily –'

'You get some rest, Mrs Matlock,' Mrs Lucas said. 'Now, Paul, have you got that school-bag packed yet?'

'Bye, Mum!' Joanna rushed out of the door with Mrs Lucas behind her.

'Bye, darling,' Flora called. 'Bring your gym-kit home tonight. Goodness knows when it was last washed.'

'Okey-dokey.' Joanna was gone.

Paul was still meticulously packing his bag.

'Your housemaster rang, darling,' Flora said. 'Any idea why?'

Paul picked up his bag and hoisted it over his shoulders. 'I'll be late for the coach, Mum.'

He started to go out of the door but Flora stopped him. 'Paul?'

'I want to board,' Paul said. 'Mr Pearson said he'd phone you to talk about it.'

'But . . . you've always hated the idea of boarding.'

'You said you'd be spending more time in London now. What's the difference?' Paul headed towards the door again.

Flora put an arm around his shoulders. 'You mean a weekly boarder? Come home at weekends?'

'*He's* here at weekends, isn't he?' Paul said, as though that settled the matter. He twisted out of her embrace and went off down the drive.

108

Flora watched him go with a feeling of terrible impending loss. When she'd first met Duncan, they had sat for hours over cheap meals, confiding in each other, the way lovers do, about everything they'd ever done or thought. He'd told her how he'd hated going to school, how much he'd missed his parents and his dogs. 'I cried so much they bought me a hamster to bribe me into going back at the end of the holidays. I called it Biscuit.'

And then, the moment Paul was born, Duncan appeared to have total amnesia about his own childhood and had begun talking about putting Paul's name down for boarding-school.

'It'll make a man of him,' he'd said.

'Eight is too young to be a man,' Flora had replied, firmly. She didn't hold with boarding-schools at any age. Her father, unable to cope with his own emotions, let alone the emotions of his twelve-year-old daughter, had taken her out of her familiar day-school and sent her off to boarding-school the week after her mother had died. Flora, already desolated by the loss of her mother, had felt totally abandoned. It was mid-term, and the girls in her class had already formed friendships and alliances. Flora, the outsider, was either teased or ignored. She'd had to work hard to be accepted. Her father told her that boarding-school would make her independent. Flora knew that it had made her manipulative and secretive. She didn't want her son to be either of these things.

During the weekend, Flora hardly had a sighting of Duncan. He was either in his study phoning useful contacts to push forward his Bill, or down at constituency headquarters humouring the local party workers.

'You did get on to the Council about the day nursery?' Flora had said over Sunday breakfast.

'Day nursery?' Duncan, who hadn't given it a thought, noticed Flora's concerned expression and said, 'Oh, that. Yes, of course. Weeks ago.'

'So, it's gone to committee?'

'Bound to have done by now,' Duncan said. 'What's up with Paul? He's looking a bit down in the dumps.'

'Not surprising, is it? Flora said. 'He wants to board, Duncan.'

'Best thing for him,' Duncan said. 'It was beginning to worry me, his clawing dependency on you. Verging on the unhealthy.' He had picked up his *Sunday Times* then, and hadn't seen the anger in Flora's face.

He'd kissed her lightly on the cheek as he left on Sunday evening. 'You haven't forgotten the Christian Wives' lunch?' he'd said. 'Wednesday.'

'No, I haven't forgotten the Christian Wives,' Flora replied.

'Good old Flora,' Duncan said. 'We're counting on you there, you know. Sir Donald is adamant that the wretched Clegg woman should be nobbled.'

At Wednesday lunchtime Flora was sitting at the high table in the banqueting hall of the Swan Hotel, under a banner reading 'Conservative Christian Wives' Association.' She was looking down on a series of long tables crammed with women dressed in sensible suits and inconsistently frivolous hats. Most of the women were looking up at Flora, who had become adept at deflecting avid stares.

She had been placed next to Veronica Weston, Chairman of the CCWA, who had kept up a lively dissertation on the virtues of Margaret Thatcher through the asparagus soup (rightly identified by Flora as packet), the Sole Bonne Femme (wrongly diagnosed by Flora as cardboard) and the fruit salad, which everyone could tell was tinned.

By the time the waitresses were threading their way around the hall with coffee and cheese biscuits, Flora had gone into a trance. She was remembering the time when the headmistress had called the whole school into the hall and announced that somebody had been guilty of stuffing a used sanitary towel behind the radiator in the locker room. 'That girl knows who she is,' Miss Phillips had said, scouring the hall with razor-sharp eyes. It hadn't been Flora, of course. But she had blushed and everyone had looked at her. Nothing, she was thinking, not even all these women staring at me and speculating on my sex-life, can ever be as miserable and petty as boarding-school. She looked up, startled, aware that Mrs Weston had ceased extolling Mrs Thatcher and was on her feet.

'The good news,' she was saying, 'is that the plans for the craft centre have now been submitted for approval. I'd like to thank our executive committee, Mrs Clegg, Mrs Hewitt, Mrs Kemp and Mrs Matlock, for their unstinting endeavours on our behalf.' There was a polite scattering of applause from the assembled women. 'And now,' Mrs Weston continued, 'we have a change from our programme of events. Mrs Matlock has asked to address us.' She smiled down at Flora encouragingly. 'Mrs Matlock?'

Flora rose. The microphone was passed along the table to her. She knew exactly what she was going to say, but she cleared her throat nervously.

'I wanted to take this chance to thank you all for your letters and messages during what, perhaps, has been the most difficult episode of my life,' she began, eliciting a murmur of sympathy laced with admiration. 'As you know, the local party decided to support my husband, and I'm grateful for their loyalty and the crucial part I know many of you played behind the scenes.' Flora paused here; she was looking directly at Rosalind Clegg at the head of the table, as she said: 'I also know there are those of you here today who initially opposed that support. I want to tell those people, here and now, that I sympathise with that view. Perhaps, for a while, I even endorsed it.' Rosalind Clegg looked keenly at Flora; she was having some difficulty following her drift. 'If it is selfish to put your family and marriage before a political career, then I am selfish,' Flora said. 'If it is selfish to want your husband at your side, as a father for your children, then – yes, I am selfish in the extreme. But . . .' She allowed herself another dramatic pause. 'But . . . through the wisdom of you ladies, I came to see that, important though the family is, the real issue here is one of duty to the party. If you can lay aside your deeply-held personal, moral and ethical beliefs for the sake of the party, then so can I.' Everyone in the hall now looked as confused as Mrs Clegg. 'I am just sorry,' Flora said, 'that the party only seems to turn to us in a crisis.' She smiled guilelessly around the room. 'How many times, I wonder, have I told my husband not to dismiss us as a bunch of tittering women in silly hats.' Mrs Clegg was now openly scowling, and there was a mutter of supressed irritation. 'I think Margaret Thatcher politicised all of us.' Flora's manner became oratorical. 'What we are all waiting for is the chance to demonstrate that. To prove our value to the party. If there is a stand to be made, we will make it. If there is talk of duty, *we* will define where our duty lies. We will show them that we ladies are truly not for turning. Thank you.'

There was a small, perplexed hush as everyone pondered Flora's meaning. And then, a young, hatless woman started to clap in rapturous applause. Gradually, all the women joined in. Rosalind Clegg rose to her feet, in an ovation. Everyone, taking her cue, rose to their feet, clapping. Flora didn't think she was imagining the occasional 'Bravo!' She sat down, flushed, smiling modestly in mute embarrassment.

As they were leaving the hall, Rosalind Clegg appeared at Flora's side. 'A moment, my dear?'

Flora turned, smiling, and Mrs Clegg gripped her hand and squeezed it. 'You've given us a lot of food for thought, Flora.'

'I'm not very good off the cuff, I'm afraid,' Flora said ingenuously.

'Oh, you made perfect sense,' Mrs Clegg said. 'Your strength has made me see my own weakness.' She released Flora's hand and looked at her significantly. 'I intend to remedy that.'

Outside the Swan Hotel, a group of assorted women and children, mostly in push-chairs, and looking as though they had just dropped in from a New Age commune, were banging tambourines, playing recorders and chanting: 'Our children need child-care . . . make our MP care.'

Groups of Christian Wives scuttled past the demonstration towards their cars, but Flora stopped to examine the banners. 'SAVE OUR NURSERY!' one read. 'DON'T LET TORY CALLOUSNESS CLOSE US!' read another.

'There she is!' Flora turned round to see Margot and Suzie, rattling their collection boxes. They rushed over to her. 'Did he do it yet?' Margot said. 'Get us scheduled at the Council meeting?'

'I understand he has,' Flora said. 'He says he has.'

'We called the Council on Monday,' said Suzie.

'It's not even on the agenda,' said Margot.

'I'll phone my husband today,' Flora said. 'I give you my word.'

'It's not your word which is in doubt, Mrs Matlock,' said Margot.

The two women rejoined the demo and Flora got into her car. At the rear of the protesters, she noticed a child with cerebral palsy. He was being pushed in a wheel-chair by one of the nursery workers.

Flora felt sickened, knowing that Duncan had been too busy saving his own skin to bother about these children who so badly needed his help. She pulled out her mobile phone and dialled his number.

His secretary answered. 'He's in a meeting, Mrs Matlock,' she said. 'He said no calls.'

'Tell him it's me,' said Flora. 'That it's urgent constituency business. I have to talk to him.'

'Hold on a minute then, will you?' said the secretary.

Flora looked at the boy with cerebral palsy and contrasted him with her own healthy children. She wondered if she would have been able to cope with such a tragedy.

Duncan's secretary came back on the phone. 'He said no exceptions, Mrs Matlock, I'm sorry. Can I get him to call you when he's –'

Flora angrily disconnected the phone, located her Filofax, and stabbed out another number.

'*Carlingham Chronicle*,' said the switchboard operator.

'Geoff Sykes, please,' said Flora.

'I'm sorry,' the operator said, 'the editor is in conference.'

'Then get him out of the conference,' Flora said. 'Tell him Flora Matlock needs to speak to him urgently. I've got a story for him.'

Flora remembered the smell. Institutional polish with under-lying traces of gym-shoes and overcooked greens. On top of this, Carlingham College followed the old school rule that no matter how freezing the classrooms and the pupils inside them, the radiators in the airless front hall must pump out a ceaseless dry, dusty heat. She felt sick, but she knew it wasn't just the atmosphere. Her stomach was churning; she had that old going-back-to-school feeling. But this time, she was

114

delivering her son to boarding-school. She was finding it very difficult to control her emotions.

They were sitting on a bench in the oak-panelled hall, waiting to see Mr Pearson. The sombre lighting, the heavy, gilt-framed portraits of ex-headmasters and the brass-bound wooden panel with the names of Old Carlingtons who died in the 1914–18 war, exuded an atmosphere of privilege and scholarship and doom. A group of small boys pounded past, on the way from the art class to their form room. They were all dressed in identical uniforms and they were all carrying identical paper painted boats; the sight of them filled Flora with melancholy. She turned to look at Paul, bespectacled yet resolute, hunched beside her. He looked so vulnerable it made her ache. She reached out to take his hand.

'Mum!' he said, tugging his hand away, embarrassed.

This upset Flora even more and they sat, for a moment, in silence, before she said: 'You won't always feel this way, you know. About Daddy.' Paul didn't reply to this, and Flora said tentatively: 'What I mean is . . . feelings can change.'

'What? Forgive and forget, like you have,' said Paul.

'Oh, I'll never forget,' Flora said, more harshly than she'd intended. She tried again. 'Anger can eat you up, you see. You have learn to use it. To build on it. Or else it destroys you.'

Paul looked at his mother curiously. Flora was on the verge of tears. 'Just one hug?' she said. Paul allowed her to put her arms around him. 'Did I ever tell you, you're the best?' Flora said. 'The very, very best.'

'And you're the second very best,' said Paul, worrying that either he or his mum was going to cry at any moment.

'Hold on,' Flora said. She reached into her pocket and handed Paul a coin. 'Your lucky coin. You mustn't forget that.'

'Mrs Matlock. Paul.' Mr Pearson had been hovering tactfully, waiting for them to disengage.

'Mr Pearson.' Flora took his hand and looked up pleadingly. 'You will take care of him, won't you? Precious cargo, and so on.'

'Don't you worry, Mrs Matlock.' Mr Pearson gave a bracing smile. 'He'll be tickety-boo. Right, Paul?'

Paul nodded. He and Mr Pearson picked up Paul's suitcases and bags and went upstairs together.

Flora sobbed all the way home. The house felt empty. Upstairs, in Paul's deserted and desolate bedroom, it felt even emptier. Mrs Lucas had stripped the bunk-bed. All Paul's personal bits and pieces had gone, his pinboard was bare. In the waste-bin, full of discarded rubbish, Flora saw the photograph of Paul and Duncan in the garden. It had been torn into pieces.

That afternoon, Sir Donald Frazier was sitting in his office reading the newspapers, and occasionally looking out of the window to enjoy the sight of a dredger moving slowly up the Thames, when he received a phone call from Flora Matlock.

'Flora, my dear,' he said. 'How are you?'

'Fine,' Flora said. 'I just called to tell you that I did the deed with Rosalind Clegg.'

'And all went smoothly?'

'Oh, I think she sees where her duty lies.'

Sir Donald smiled approvingly. 'I think we're all beginning to see that, my dear.'

He was about to sign off and put down the phone when Flora suddenly said: 'How are the leaders going?'

Sir Donald glanced at the newspapers on his desk. '*The Times* was particularly sanctimonious. All in all, though, the story is showing distinct signs of metal fatigue.'

'So the Bill wasn't an issue?' Flora said.

'No,' Sir Donald replied. 'He's ahead on all fronts, I'd say.'

'Thanks to you.'

Sir Donald returned the compliment. 'You were the ballast, my dear.'

There was, he thought, a tremor in Flora's voice as she said, 'I don't know why your good opinion of me is so vital, Donald. But it is. Terribly.'

She hung up before he could say anything. Just as well, he thought to himself, putting down the phone. He couldn't imagine what would have been the correct response. He gazed thoughtfully at the dredger, feeling mildly flattered that he was still capable of arousing such a depth of feeling in a young woman like Flora Matlock. Yet he was puzzled by it also. As if there had been a subtle change in their relationship, without him being aware of it.

13

Flora had just been to Waitrose for the weekly shop and bought a giant packet of Coco Pops and a tub of butterscotch ice-cream, Paul's two favourite foods – preferably served one on top of the other. She just couldn't get used to the idea of him not being around.

As she turned into her drive, glumly counting the weeks until the end of term, a young man in a battered Barbour jumped out of an equally battered Ford Escort and opened the gates. Flora, recognising the reporter who lived at the bottom of her garden, opened the car window and leaned out.

'Thank you, Mr . . . ?'

'Montford,' he said. 'Alan Montford.'

'Thank you, Mr Montford. We were wondering, the children and I, if you were planning to take up permanent residence outside our gates?'

'Well, the thing is,' said the reporter, 'a couple of the nationals are paying me a retainer to stick around just in case –'

'Of what?' Flora interrupted. 'I should have thought you'd all had your pound of flesh.'

'Oh, steady on,' said Alan Montford. 'I'm just the tip-off man. Mostly I work for the *Chronicle*, not the *Sun*. As a matter of fact, I was hoping to have a brief word?' Flora switched off the ignition. 'I was in the *Chronicle* yesterday,' he said. 'Lovely human-interest piece they've got for the front page this week.'

'It's a good paper,' Flora said.

'I was saying to Geoff, the editor, I wouldn't be surprised if that story didn't turn out political dynamite.'

'Really?' Flora switched on the ignition. 'Well . . .'

Alan Montford rested an elbow on the open window. 'Naturally, Geoff wouldn't name his sources.'

'If you'll excuse me.' Flora moved to close the electric window.

Alan put out a restraining hand. 'All I wanted to say was that I've got a hot line to the nationals if anyone –'

'I'll tell my husband.' Flora put the car into gear. 'Now, would you be awfully kind and shut the gates after me?'

The telephone was ringing and Flora, who had just had a bath, slipped on her towelling robe and went into the bedroom to answer it.

It was Duncan, phoning from the office. 'I'm leaving now, lovely,' he said. 'Traffic allowing, I'll be home about eight.'

'Lovely'? As Flora put down the phone she heard again Jennifer Caird saying: 'When can you leave?' Duncan saying: 'In an hour, lovely. Traffic allowing, I'll be at your flat about eight.'

There was only one tape left. Flora took it from a drawer and slipped it into the stereo cassette. After this, she thought, I'll bin the lot of them.

Duncan was speaking on the tape. He sounded desperate. 'I just can't make it, there's no way. That slag of a secretary didn't put the meeting in my diary.'

'Oh, Duncan.' Jennifer was obviously disappointed.

'I'll make it up to you, lovely, I swear.' Flora looked ruefully out of the window. She couldn't remember Duncan ever needing her with such urgent intensity.

'When? You'll be off home for the weekend tomorrow.'

'Now, then. Right now. Are you wearing it. The black number?'

'Oh, Duncan, don't even think about it.'

'Put your fingers through the slit . . .'

The intimate voices of her husband and his mistress fuelled Flora with nihilistic, erotic emotions. Hardly aware of what she was doing, she went over to the curtains and drew them, then took Duncan's present, the black silk underwear, out of the chest of drawers, put it on and lay down on the bed.

Duncan was saying: 'Put your fingers on our spot marked X. Do it, lovely.' And Flora was drawing up her legs, putting her fingers through the slit in the silk.

Jennifer cried: 'Tell me, tell me what to do . . .'

'Ever so gently, now,' Duncan said softly. 'Tease it out. Ease it out. That's my little girl, my little tiger.'

'Ohh . . . Oh God.'

'I'm with you, baby. I'm in there, lovely. I've got you in the palm of my hand.'

'Oh, Duncan, oh my darling . . .' Jennifer cried out.

'Oh, Duncan.' Flora sobbed, despairingly.

'Now two fingers. Three if you can. And harder. Tough love, remember? Hard as you like. Hard as you can stand it.'

'Oh . . . yes . . . oh, God forgive me . . .' Jennifer sobbed.

Flora had closed her eyes, to lose herself in sensual pleasure.

'Stay with it, Jenny. Hit the spot. Our spot. Do it for me, baby.'

'Oh no . . . oh please,' Jennifer cried out.

Suddenly Flora, gripped by the brutal realisation of what she was doing, froze, filled with self-repugnance.

'Here we go, sweetheart. Here comes the roller coaster. Up and over we go . . .'

Jennifer moaned as she reached a climax. Flora rolled over in bed, curled in anguish, covering her ears with her hands.

Five . . . ten minutes later, she got up from the bed, tore off the cami-knickers, and pushed them into the back of the drawer. Then she went into the bathroom and ran another bath. Hot and cleansing.

She was setting the table in the dining-room, dressed and composed, when she heard Duncan's car sweep into the drive. Joanna was messing about with her bike on the terrace outside the dining-room window, and Flora watched her chuck the bicycle aside and run to greet her father. Duncan swept her up into his arms as Mark Hollister got out of the car, carrying Duncan's red boxes. He glanced up at the house and saw Flora at the window. They looked at each other, but neither of them smiled or waved.

Duncan was lying in the bath, checking over some papers and speaking into his dictaphone. 'Para three, page nine should read "in the light of these statistics it was agreed etc." '

Flora, down in the hall, heard him yell for Mark. She waited until Mark had gone upstairs before slipping into Duncan's study. Briskly, she pulled some papers out of one of the red boxes on his desk, checked them and put them through the fax machine.

She was out of the study and on her way to the kitchen when she heard Duncan shouting imperiously over the running water: 'I want that lot transcribed and on my desk by Monday morning, Mark. Make sure it happens.'

The kitchen table was littered with papers and Flora was riffling through them, thinking how foolishly unaware Duncan was of Mark's resentment, when Mark wandered in.

Flora, without looking up, continued sifting the papers. 'We never concluded our conversation the other day.'

'Didn't we?' Mark said.

'Is this it?' Flora indicated the papers. 'The Bill?'

Mark, smiling faintly, said: 'Another blow for the family from the Minister for the Family. It's why I'm here, fine-tuning the details. A thankless task for which one gets no gratitude, but – there you go.' He gave her a sidelong glance. 'You know how it is with him. How he colonises every idea, every suggestion, as his own? Then there's his endless gibes at gays and women. We're just not in the club, you see.'

So that's it, Flora thought. Why hadn't I realised before? 'Is that why you came to see me?'

Mark shook his head. 'Not entirely.' He appeared to be explaining it to himself as much as to Flora, as he said deliberately: 'When someone like Duncan gets control of a party it becomes infected from the top down. It can take years to cleanse itself. Some of us have worked hard to set up this Ministry; we want to prevent that.'

'Goodness,' Flora said. 'You sound like a . . . what do they call it . . . an *agent provocateur*?'

'Hardly,' Mark gave another faint smile.

'Only someone close to the throne can be that,' Flora said. 'Someone he trusts. Someone who understands attention to detail and dissemination of information.'

Mark adjusted his glasses and looked at Flora questioningly. 'And disinformation?'

'That, too.' Flora looked away, uncomfortable with their unspoken collusion. 'I was doing his surgery for him once,' she said. 'A man came in. Unemployed. His youngest child, a three-year-old boy, had just died of leukaemia. The funeral was on welfare, as it were. But when he and his wife took their other children back a week later to visit the grave, it still wasn't covered up. The coffin was just lying there, at the bottom of the hole.'

'Oh, God,' Mark said softly.

'I asked Duncan how this could happen. He said it was because the grave was not yet full. It seems three others had to be put on top of the child, before they could cover the grave. So, I wrote them a cheque.'

There was a bleak and complicated silence. Mark shuffled the papers together and then put them back on the table, neatly squaring the pile. 'I really should be more careful about leaving this stuff lying around,' he said. 'God knows what damage could be done if it got into the wrong hands.'

Duncan was still in his bath, luxuriating in frothy Radox, as Flora came in with a whisky and the local paper. 'You're a mind-reader,' he said, reaching out for the whisky.

Flora put the *Chronicle* on the bath stool, picked up a sponge and, perching on the side of the bath, started gently scrubbing his back.

'How went it at the school?' Duncan asked.

'Oh, you know Paul,' said Flora. 'He never shows much.'

'It's the best thing for him,' said Duncan. 'He gets mollycoddled here – all you women.'

Flora made a conscious effort not to rise to this. 'Why did Mark come this weekend?'

'More bloody work on the Bill,' Duncan said. 'It never ends.'

'I should really be briefed on it, you know, Duncan.' Flora sponged soapily between his shoulder-blades. 'If only to cover the home front here.'

Duncan sipped his whisky, feeling totally relaxed. 'Child Benefit has always been a hot potato,' he said, 'but the bloody manifesto locked us into keeping it. It does not, however, prohibit us from privatising it.'

'So?' Flora gently massaged his back.

'Okay,' Duncan said. 'Point one. All those entitled to claim are free to continue doing so. Point two, and this is the incentive, all those who choose to opt out will enter a scheme whereby for the first five years of their child's life, the Government will invest the money on their behalf in a specially constructed, high interest investment scheme.'

'And after the five years?'

'You receive education vouchers for the school of your choice. Humdinger, isn't it? By involving the private sector, we can turn the whole damned thing over to the insurance companies and building societies. And those who do go on claiming Child benefit can collect it from a hole in the wall.'

Flora pensively digested the implications of all this and Duncan, mistaking her expression for admiration, said: 'Really innovative legislation always comes from the vision of one man.'

'Even if you do say so yourself.' Flora smiled and took a sip from Duncan's whisky.

'You're one of the few people I dare say it to, my darling.' Duncan was warmed by his bath and her admiration. 'And that's not all,' he added eagerly. 'This is where the real saving lies. And it's a honey. I tell you, the PM practically broke into a tap dance. Those mothers who continue claiming the benefit will receive a monthly cash bonus from the Government, providing – and this is the clincher – providing they contract to stay at home and look after the kids for the first five years. The old robbing Peter principle.'

'So you don't have to go to the ridiculous expense of providing nation-wide nursery care?'

'Exactly. Mind you, we'll have to swing it through the House like we did the Child Support Agency thing. If we stop to draw breath, we'll be nuked.' Duncan caught Flora's hand

124

and kissed the inside of her wrist. 'I forget how soft your skin is. Baby soft.' He kissed it again. 'Velveteen soft.'

Flora left her hand in his. 'What you need is the right input, darling. From the insurance side. Someone you can really trust. I'm just thinking aloud here . . . Marlborough Insurance . . . when you were on the Board there must have been someone . . . I mean, someone the wets would really buy?' She waited, letting the question hover.

'There's Martin Pryce,' Duncan said doubtfully.

'Perfect,' said Flora.

'Bit close to home, sweetheart. You know what an echo chamber the House is.'

'He'd be quite an ally.'

Duncan digested this. 'Unless we had him and Peggy over to dinner here? Strictly informal? Who's to know?'

'He's always been such a fan,' Flora said. 'It's not as if he'd expect anything in return.'

Duncan, touched by her advice and insight, pulled Flora to him and kissed her. 'You always think the best of people, don't you? It's a knack I seem to have lost.'

Flora pulled back, feeling a disquieting twinge of disloyalty.

'Why don't you take your clothes off?' Duncan said. 'Hop in?' Flora made no move to co-operate. 'You can't still have the wretched curse?'

'No, I . . .'

'Well, then?' He cupped her face in his wet hands and kissed her again.

The phone rang. Flora gratefully disengaged herself and hurried into the bedroom to answer it.

'Shit!' Duncan said and felt a flash of irritation as he heard Flora say: 'Paul! Darling! How's it all going?'

He picked up the *Carlingham Chronicle* from the stool next to the bath and casually scanned the front page. Almost immediately he was brought up short by a half-page picture of the nursery demo. A child with cerebral palsy was sitting in a wheelchair at the front of the group. Duncan read the banner headline, 'MATLOCK'S MARTYRS', and flung the paper aside. 'Shit! Shit! Shit!' he said.

Mark Hollister darted into the Members' toilet in the House of Commons, looked around furtively, checked that the urinals were empty and then, taking his mobile phone out of his pocket, quickly dialled a number. He was well aware that he was behaving like the chief spy or major mole in a John le Carré movie, and was enjoying himself almost as much as if he were playing the role to camera. If he hadn't been a bright, upwardly-mobile scholarship boy, Mark thought, he might have become an actor instead of a disenchanted civil servant.

There was no answer. Putting away his mobile, he was wondering nervously whether Flora was absolutely reliable, when it rang and she came on the line.

'It's me.'

'I've been trying to get you,' Mark said. 'Have we got a date?'

'Next Friday. Our man is Alan Montford.' She gave Mark two Carlingham telephone numbers. 'Home and mobile, in that order. Okay?'

'Right,' said Mark. 'I'll set things in motion.' He pressed the off-button on his phone and promptly re-dialled.

In the bathroom at Mindermere House, Flora caught sight of herself in the mirror and hardly recognised the flushed and excited face looking back at her. The phone went again, almost immediately. Flora assumed it was a postscript to the previous call. 'Mark?'

It wasn't Mark, but a voice Flora recognised all too easily. 'This is Jennifer Caird. I need to meet with you. To talk. As soon as possible.'

'Offhand, I can't think of a single topic we have in common, Miss Caird,' Flora said.

'Really? I can.'

'Then you're mistaken.' Flora slammed off her phone with a bravado she did not actually feel. What could Jennifer Caird possibly want to talk to her about?

Flora had parked her car behind a hedge, just beyond the perimeter fence of the Carlingham College rugby pitch. In the middle of a group of mud-smeared boys, frantic in their efforts to get possession of the ball, she could see Paul, gawky, poignantly out of place in this athletic arena.

Flora knew exactly how he felt. She'd never been able to understand why her schoolfriends enjoyed standing on the edge of a muddy field every Saturday afternoon, cheering on their house or their form. She was not a team player, never would be, and she'd hated all those grey, cold, wet afternoons with large girls hurling themselves at her, hacking at her fingers with their lacrosse sticks.

On the rugby pitch, the burly games teacher yelled and blew his whistle at the boys, whipping them into a frenzy of competition, and Flora's heart plummeted as the ball came towards Paul. His team mates were shrieking, the games master was shouting. Paul, paralysed with fear, bravely squared himself and ignited into action. Plunging after the ball, he missed it entirely and landed in the mud. An opponent grabbed it and they all streaked after him, leaving Paul lying there, crumpled in humiliation, his glasses streaked with dirt.

Flora reversed the car and drove into Carlingham to buy lilies for the dinner party the following day. She was thinking how terribly unhappy Paul must have been to willingly exchange Mindermere for compulsory Saturday games and a dormitory full of taunting boys. And Duncan was to blame.

Mrs Lucas came into the dining-room, bearing lilies floating spectacularly in a cut-glass bowl.

'Centre stage, Mrs Lucas, don't you think?' said Flora. She was wearing the Armani trouser-suit, checking the gleaming silverware and arranging place cards on the long mahogany dining table. Mrs Lucas carefully placed the bowl in the centre of the table. 'I always say, no one can arrange flowers like you do, Mrs Matlock.'

'What one might call an acquired skill,' Flora said drily. She turned to the waiter who was giving a final polish to the cutlery. 'Do you think, perhaps, the place settings are a mite cluttered?'

'I could put the mats under the cloth, madam,' the waiter said.

Flora, seeing Duncan in the hall, said, 'Darling, what do you think?'

'About what?' Duncan came into the room.

'The place settings,' Flora said. 'Would it look better with the mats under the cloth?'

'They look fine to me.' Duncan gave the table a perfunctory glance, then looked more keenly at Flora. 'That cream thing you're wearing . . . I always like you in that.'

'You've never seen me in it before,' Flora said.

'Really? I could have sworn. . . .' Duncan, vaguely sensing dangerous territory, reverted to the table: 'Have you done the placement yet?'

'Joan Patterson on your right, then Roger Gravely, Peggy Pryce, Hugo Patterson, me, Daddy, Pippa Gravely and Martin Pryce on your left,' said Flora, reading from the place cards.

'Two men together?'

128

Before Flora could point out that this was the whole point of the exercise, the doorbell was ringing, the guests arriving, and a waiter was circling the drawing room with champagne goblets.

Seated at the dinner table, in the flickering candle-light, the conversation flowed predictably. The women admired Flora's flower arrangement and the delicious food, the men talked politics. Flora caught snatches of their discussion. 'And the beauty is how it reduces dependency on the Post Offices,' her father was saying.

'Which nicely clears the way for their own privatisation,' said Roger Gravely.

Duncan grinned. 'What you'd call a double whammy.'

Martin Pryce leant forward eagerly. 'The important thing is to lay the right groundwork. Zap the nanny state advocates before they know what's hit them.'

'Exactly right,' Duncan agreed.

Flora switched off from the masculine chat as Peggy Pryce said: 'Flora, I'm so sorry Martin and I were late. We had to make this tedious detour.'

'He said, but he was rather circumspect about why,' Flora replied.

'You know Pangbourne Manor, that crumbling Victorian monstrosity beyond the bypass? The owners defaulted last year. Martin's company got hold of it. He thought it might be something we could take on ourselves.'

'And is it?' Flora asked, trying to overhear Duncan at the other end of the table.

'Some idiot has put pebble-dash all over the façade, the garden's a jungle – north-facing to boot – and the roof is like a colander. I told him, he'd practically have to give the damn thing away.'

Flora was now wholly absorbed in what Peggy was

saying. 'Tell you what, Peggy. Why don't we have lunch together very soon?'

The evening was a success and, as the guests tumbled out of the front door, mellowed with good wine and goodwill, Martin linked his arm with Flora's and said quietly: 'You're all right, then?'

'Oh, we're through the worst now,' Flora said. 'Forward thrust, as Daddy would say.'

'Good on you.' Martin squeezed her arm. 'You did the right thing, you know, Flora. Sticking by him. It's you who grounds him, who gives him his bearings. He told me so himself.' He didn't notice Flora's regretful expression as he put his arm around her to kiss her goodnight: 'Well, my love, it's been a wonderful . . .'

Duncan came over to them and jokingly tapped Martin on the shoulder. 'Unhand my wife, sir!'

'Gad, sir, I hope that's not a threat, sir!' Martin replied, striking a martial pose.

The two of them laughingly shadow-boxed each other, the uninhibited horseplay of two old friends. Suddenly they were startled by flashing lights.

Clive, on the steps behind them, peered up the drive. 'What the . . . ?'

'It's a flashlight,' Duncan said. 'A fucking camera flashlight.'

'But who?' Peggy was also looking up the drive.

'The Press, one assumes,' Clive said.

They heard a car start up, and as the engine noise receded, Flora said, 'Whoever it is they've gone.'

'Opportunistic bastards,' Duncan said.

'Does it happen often?' Peggy Pryce asked.

'Often enough, I'm afraid,' said Flora. Seeing the anger in Duncan's face she added: 'Don't let it sour the evening, darling. I doubt if they got much.'

Flora was already in bed and Duncan, looking moodily out of the window into the night, was on the telephone. 'No, no,' he was saying irritably. 'All those wankers at the Press Complaints Commission ever do is rap their knuckles after the event. I want ou to find out which of the frenzied feeders it is and get back to me.'

'Mark,' he explained, taking off his dressing-gown and getting into bed. 'Seems I woke him, but that's what he's paid for.'

Flora kissed him lightly and turned her back, snuggling down to sleep. Duncan lay there for a moment, and then said: 'Is something going on with you, Flora?' She looked back at him, without a word. 'You seem so . . . I don't know . . . distant.' She said nothing to this, either. He rolled her over to face him. 'I want so much for us to be close.'

Flora was touched by the genuine urgency in his voice, but scared by the realisation that he was still able to reach her emotionally.

He started unbuttoning her nightdress. 'Where's that little wild-cat? That little tiger I unleashed last time? God, you were a turn-on.' He moved to kiss her breasts. Flora, overwhelmed by a sudden flash of anger, quickly rolled around so that she was on top of him, pinning his arms.

Duncan grinned up at her. 'That's more like it. That's my girl.'

She switched off the light, consumed by a complexity of emotions. 'You're an utter bastard, Duncan,' she said, slapping him, hard and stingingly, on the cheek.

For no more than a second, Duncan was taken aback by the force of the blow. And then he smiled. 'Yes. Oh, yes, my love. Yes. Again.'

Flora struck him again. As he moved to kiss her breasts she began to weep silently. His own sexual humiliation was somehow her own. Then he started to go down on her. 'Let

131

me taste you. Please? Let me come home?' As he went down she felt a terrible fusion of ecstasy and pain. She shouted aloud in a moan of despair and self-loathing at the sensual pleasure he was giving her. Then she surrendered herself to the darkness of her climax.

There was a For Sale sign at the end of the drive leading up to Pangbourne Manor. Flora drove past, pulled up and looked at the house. Peggy had been right. It was crumbling, but there was still a touch of decaying elegance behind the neglected Victorian façade.

She looked at it speculatively for a moment, and then she reached for her phone and dialled a number. 'Mark? Can you talk?'

'Briefly,' Mark replied.

'Put a hold on the pictures,' Flora said. 'I may have something more. The icing on the cake.'

Clive and Flora were sitting on the terrace at Mindermere House, watching Joanna playing on the swing.

'She must miss Paul,' Clive said.

'It's Duncan she misses. She was always a Daddy's girl, right from the start,' Flora said. 'Paul was mine.'

Clive risked a quick look at Flora's expression and said: 'Hey, steady on, old girl. He'll do just fine.'

Flora sat there, staring at nothing, trying to articulate her thoughts. 'Schools like that, they define you, don't they? Mould you? That's the whole idea.'

'Which is just why it'll be the making of him. I know mine was.'

Flora longed to point out that if her father's school had been the making of him, then they hadn't made a very good job of it; handicapping him for life with the notion that it was unmanly to have emotions. She remembered that when her mother was dying, Clive had stopped her going to the hospital. 'Leave it to the professionals, Flo. The doctors know what they're doing.' She'd been sent to stay with an aunt while her father took care of the funeral arrangements and when she got home it was as if her mother had never existed. Her sewing box had gone from the corner of the sitting-room, the enamelled brush and comb set was missing from the dressing-table and there were no clothes in her wardrobe. Only her jewellery had been kept for Flora. 'I've put it in the bank for safe-keeping,' Clive had said.

Recent events had made Flora look at her father from a new and disconcerting perspective. There had always been a chasm of communication between them. Now she knew it was unbridgeable.

She picked up a manilla envelope lying on the terrace table and passed it to her father. Clive opened it, puzzled. 'Pangbourne Manor, Flora? What's this all about?'

'Martin Pryce's insurance company owns it,' Flora said. 'I got Peggy to speak to him for me. He'll let me have it for under half the valued price, Daddy.' She managed to look eager and yet anxious for his approval.

Clive quickly scanned the estate agent's details. 'It's a white elephant, Flora. Any surveyor would blow it out of the water.'

'Mother left that money in trust for both of us,' Flora said firmly. 'I've never asked before.' This unaccustomed mention of her mother silenced Clive. 'Martin says if I get my act together, we can exchange by next week. Just think, Daddy. All those bedrooms. There'll come a time when you can't go on living alone. One must try to plan ahead . . .'

She's full of surprises today, Clive thought. 'Duncan might have a view on that,' he said doubtfully.

'He doesn't know anything about it,' Flora said. 'I want to surprise him. You know how fond he is of you, Daddy. He hasn't forgotten what you did for him. Your exercise in damage control with the Press.' She couldn't resist adding, 'I haven't forgotten either, Daddy.' Realising she might have gone too far, she softened her tone: 'He's more like a son to you than any real son could ever be, isn't he? Or daughter, come to that.'

'It's not a competition, Flora,' Clive said.

Flora looked over at Joanna, playing on the swing. Clive was following her gaze, as she knew he would. 'I worry sometimes,' she said, 'that when Duncan finally reaches the Olympian heights in Westminster, we'll lose him. You of all people don't deserve that, Daddy. Which is why I thought your name should be on the deeds. That way you'll have a real stake in the future, you'll be part of it with us. Right down the line.'

Clive, still looking fondly at his granddaughter, said: 'It's an interesting idea, Flo. I'll have to think about it.'

Flora linked her arm in his. 'Don't take too long, Daddy. The clock is running.'

14

Mark Hollister was standing at the end of the passage connecting the House of Lords with the Commons, watching Colin Fletcher and Ian Ruby-Smith, huddled together over some papers. Colin was talking agitatedly; Ian was looking surreptitiously over his shoulder. They exchanged a few more muttered words and then Ian headed off in one direction and Colin walked briskly towards Mark.

'Colin?' Mark stepped out of the shadows.

Colin pulled up abruptly. 'Oh, it's you, Mark. I've just got this fax.' He thrust the papers at Mark. 'They're running it tomorrow, would you believe?'

Mark studied the papers. 'Jesus.' He exhaled slowly. 'It'll be a bloody miracle if we ride this one out.'

They were walking down the Commons corridor now, past the committee rooms. Duncan was ahead of them, talking to a group of MPs. 'So, who's going to spread the glad tidings?' Colin said.

'You're his Head of Information.' Mark handed Colin the papers and hung back.

Colin sighed heavily. 'Well, here goes.' He loitered discreetly on the edge of the group of MPs, trying to catch Duncan's eye. Eventually, Duncan saw him and followed him into a secluded alcove under a stained-glass window.

'So much for our bloody legal boys.' Colin handed Duncan the papers. 'They're running it tomorrow.'

Duncan looked at the photographs of Pangbourne Manor – one of them with his father-in-law beside it – and shook his head, totally perplexed. 'It makes no sense. Where the hell is this Pangbourne Manor, anyway?'

'Somewhere in your neck of the woods, apparently.' Someone passed in the corridor and Colin stepped swiftly in front of Duncan to shield him from view.

Duncan's tone was dismissive. 'There's going to be a lot of egg on a lot of faces if they think –'

Colin interrupted. 'Read on.'

Something in Colin's voice caused Duncan to turn the page quickly. He could not believe what he saw there. A photograph of himself and Martin Pryce, frozen like rabbits caught in the headlights of a car, shadow boxing in front of Mindermere House.

'Good God,' Duncan said through clenched teeth. He strode off towards his office carrying the papers. Colin followed more slowly.

'Well?' Mark said, catching him up.

'I swear he didn't know a thing about it,' Colin said. 'Or he's a better bloody actor than we think he is.'

There was a flurry of activity in Duncan's office. As Mark and Colin joined the rest of the team, they could see Duncan through the glass walls of his inner sanctum. He was striding up and down, speaking agitatedly into his portable phone. He was talking to his father-in-law.

'You stupid, stupid old man,' he was saying. 'Do you have any idea what you've done?'

Clive, who had been sitting comfortably by the fire listening to *The Archers*, was startled by the venom in Duncan's voice. 'What . . . what have I done?'

'Pangbourne Manor. Why the hell didn't you discuss it with me?' Duncan was hissing with a malicious anger born out of fear. 'You lock your door and put your answering machine on and do nothing . . . nothing, do you hear me? Not so much as a fart until I give you the word. You're an

136

amateur, Clive. I let you in too close. And that's a mistake I won't make again.'

Duncan hung up and dialled another number. 'Jeremy . . . ?' Mark, observing Duncan through the glass wall, thought he looked like a man desperately clinging to the rock-face by his nails.

The following morning, Clive, in his pyjamas, unshaven and bloated with apprehension, was watching breakfast television. A sharp-looking political pundit was holding forth about Duncan. 'So Duncan Matlock is once again headline news. This time the scandal is not sexual, but political. The sale of Pangbourne Manor to a close relative – the purchaser is his father-in-law – is not in itself significant. But the knockdown sale price does have a clear element of gift about it.'

Clive groaned, aware of his own unwitting culpability. Flora . . . Flora would know. He must get on to Flora. He pulled himself up from the armchair and then clutched his throat, slumping back in the chair. 'Flora . . . ?' His eyes widened in appalled comprehension.

'. . . the fact that the vendor is Marlborough Insurance adds another dimension to the story, particularly in view of the leak about Duncan Matlock's proposed Bill to privatise Child Benefit and the key role insurance companies are expected to play in this . . .'

Duncan, in his London flat, was also watching breakfast television. He was sitting on the edge of his bed, unshaven, in pyjamas and dressing-gown, surrounded by a panoply of morning papers. His face was gaunt with anxiety.

'. . . before becoming a Member of Parliament, Duncan Matlock was on the Board of Directors of Marlborough Insurance and his friendship with the charismatic Chairman,

Martin Pryce, is clearly a close one. They had dinner together only a week or so ago.'

A photograph of Martin and Duncan, uninhibited and inebriated, shadow boxing outside Mindermere House, flashed onto the television. Duncan gazed at the screen and shook his head in total bewilderment.

'. . . in the light of his highly sensitive Bill on privatising Child Benefit, this whole thing is more than just an embarrassment for Duncan Matlock. It's a potential catastrophe.'

Mrs Lucas came into the kitchen as Flora, sitting at the kitchen table, eating toast and marmalade, switched off the television set. She drained her coffee. 'Can you hold the fort for a day or two, Mrs Lucas? I have to go to London.'

In Duncan's office, a cacophony of ringing telephones were being picked up by an answering machine on the switchboard. His secretary arrived, tugged off her coat and was gazing at the ringing phones perplexedly as Duncan swung in and marched straight into the inner office, closely followed by Colin Fletcher, Mark Hollister and Ian Ruby-Smith.

'The draft Bill went to ITN last night,' Colin said. 'My chap at Fortress Wapping said the pictures and story were there yesterday at midday, hand-delivered. Ditto the *Guardian*, *Telegraph* and *Mail*.'

'So, it was an orchestrated campaign?' Duncan said.

'Down to the last detail,' said Colin.

'The theory is, it's someone at Marlborough Insurance,' said Mark. 'How else did they get all the purchase details?'

'It's someone closer to home than that.' Duncan stabbed a finger at Mark. 'Call Flora. She'll be at the flat later. Get the names of those caterers we used at the Pryce dinner party.' He turned to Ian. 'Someone tipped that photographer off, someone who knew where we'd be and when. If we can get them on a dirty tricks rap it will discredit the story.'

'And deflect the flak,' Colin said.

'How about Jeremy?' said Ian. 'Did he come up with anything?'

'I checked him out on the possibility of a "we've all learnt some useful lessons from this" statement, but he said no go.' Duncan had no intention of telling his team that what Jeremy had actually said was, 'The only lesson to be learnt from this whole bloody fiasco, Duncan, is to keep your nose clean.' He sat down at his desk and, as he scanned the morning papers, his panic increased.

His secretary put her head round the door. 'Sir Donald is still unavailable, Minister. And the Chief Whip is with the Prime Minister.'

Duncan exchanged a look with Ian. 'Keep trying until you get them,' he said.

He reverted to the papers and, half talking to himself, said: 'It's how they used to do it in Stalin's day. You put in a request for help to the party and, if the answer was no, all you got was a blanket of bloody silence.'

Mark noticed that Duncan's hands were trembling. His hold on events was starting to slip.

Pushing her way through the barrier at Euston, Flora was instantly surrounded by a group of reporters, thrusting microphones in her face.

'Does your husband have any financial interest in Marlborough Insurance?' shouted one of the reporters.

Putting her head down, Flora threaded her way through the group.

'Did you know anything about this house sale, Mrs Matlock?' said another.

'They're saying the house is a bribe, Mrs Matlock. So his

old company gets favoured treatment when his Bill gets through. Any comment on that?'

'No comment.' Flora reached the taxi rank and jumped into the first cab. 'The Ivy, please,' she said. 'West Street.'

Flora was shown to a corner table for two in the wood-panelled restaurant. She studied the other diners, who she suspected were mostly in show business or the media: they had the relaxed, self-important air of people expecting to be recognised. Flora, who wouldn't recognise Princess Diana if she came and sat down next to her, couldn't even remember what Kitty MacDonald looked like. She had only met the Party Chairman's wife twice. Firstly, at a private dinner at Bucks given by Jeremy Phipps just after Duncan had been made a Minister, when Mrs MacDonald had patronised her in the Ladies ('Charming dress, my dear. I very nearly bought it myself'). And then at a party conference in Brighton, when Flora, dancing an energetic Scottish reel, had inadvertently run her high heel down Mrs MacDonald's shin bone. Neither occasion boded well for the lunch.

But Kitty MacDonald, a large woman upholstered in a pinkish Chanel suit embellished with gold braid, a jaunty salmon-pink silk bow at her neck, exuded goodwill as she was shown to the table.

'Flora, my dear . . .' She gave Flora the caring look she had come to hate. 'I'm so glad you took me up on our lunch date.'

Flora got up to greet her. 'Mrs MacDonald. I'm just sorry I've been so long getting back to you.'

Mrs MacDonald smiled understandingly. 'You've had more on your mind than lunching with me.' She settled heavily onto the banquette and patted the place next to her. 'And it's Kitty, dear. Call me Kitty.'

They ordered a bottle of house white and studied the menu. 'Ah, fish-cakes,' Kitty said. 'Don't you love them?'

They chatted for a while about how restaurant fish-cakes

were never really quite as good as the ones you made at home, and moved on through innocuous conversations about their children during the first course. It was over the fruit salad that Kitty got down to business.

'We're all so grateful you stayed firm, Flora,' she said. 'The party can't afford to lose women like you.'

'Thank you, Kitty,' Flora said.

'Many of us have been through it, you know. Powerful men are always a temptation to silly young girls, but if you're wise, like you've been, Flora, you get on with your life – the garden, the charity work, the children – and wait for them to come home. They always do, you know.'

'Always?'

'Oh, yes,' Kitty said. 'You see, my dear, these trivial affairs mean nothing. The love between a husband and wife – now, that's different. That's a special kind of love.'

'Isn't that just emotional band-aid?' said Flora. 'It may cover up the wound for a while but it doesn't heal anything.'

'Ah, you're hurt.' Kitty said. 'I can understand that.'

'I was hurt,' Flora corrected her. 'Now I'm cured. It's poor Duncan I'm worried about.'

'Duncan?' Kitty looked surprised.

'He seems to have gone to pieces,' said Flora. 'Guilt, I suppose.' She ordered coffee for them both. 'The business this morning, for instance . . .'

'This morning?' Kitty said. 'I don't think I'm quite with you?'

It occurred to Flora that Kitty MacDonald could not have read the newspapers or looked at the television before she left home. 'He's got himself involved in some scandal to do with an insurance company. They say he's been bribed.'

'I can't believe it,' Kitty said. 'He wouldn't be so foolish.'

'That's just it. It's so unlike Duncan. I'm afraid he may be heading for a breakdown.'

'And he's got to pilot his Bill through the House.'

'Exactly,' said Flora. 'That's why I'd so value your advice.'

'You shall have it.' Kitty raised her chin resolutely. 'And rest assured that anything you tell me will be totally in confidence.' She sipped her coffee and waited avidly for Flora to begin. She was wondering whether her husband would be at party headquarters this afternoon or in his Whitehall office.

Flora was in the flat, putting a bottle of champagne into the ice-bucket, when she heard a noise behind her. She started and turned. The flat door was being opened with a key. Flora froze in fear.

'Don't worry, I came in the back way.' Jennifer Caird walked calmly into the kitchen and dropped the key onto the table. 'I should have returned it before. Sorry about that.' Flora was momentarily too surprised to speak. 'I guessed you'd be here to hold his hand.' She met Flora's eyes. 'It's bad, isn't it?'

'Yes,' Flora said. 'It's bad.'

'Poor bastard,' Jennifer said.

Flora looked at Jennifer for a moment and saw genuine concern in her face. 'Say what it is you want, Miss Caird. I have things to do.'

'I want my entry card back,' Jennifer said. 'All those invisible doors you closed against me? I want them opened.' She wandered into the sitting-room, pensively fingering the familiar objects.

Flora followed her. 'You've had your fifteen minutes of fame.'

'I could have had a full calendar year if I'd wished it,' Jennifer said, with spirit. 'All Alistair Drummond wanted was the money. I could have gone down that road with him. I could have got myself a publicity agent, spread my legs and laughed all the way to the bank, as he did. I didn't. I laid low. I did that for Duncan. That was *my* damage control. It was the sex that did it for us. He always said one day it would devour us.'

Flora, who had almost been warming to Jennifer Caird, now gazed at her coldly. 'And you've come to claim your reward?'

'I'm not a fool, Flora,' Jennifer said. 'I couldn't take your place, I'd never get past the selection committee. We both know that.' She looked out through the window at the roofs of Westminster. 'He told me you hated it. Politics, the House. Like Norma Major. At the beginning she always looked as though she was longing to get back to her home in the sticks. Me, I love it. I like being the only girl in a boys' school. That's power, too, in its own way.'

Flora was aware that she was not dealing with one of Kitty MacDonald's silly little girls. 'And you want it back?' Jennifer nodded. 'Not within my providence, I'm afraid,' Flora said.

'Oh, come on,' said Jennifer. 'A flick through the old Filofax, call up a few contacts. How about a statement of public forgiveness in *Femail*? The lifting of the blockade. It would take half a morning on the phone – if that. You know the angle. "I suppose she loved him, in her way. I have to remind myself that she was very young." '

Flora found it hard to believe that Jennifer Caird was actually smiling at her as she outlined this extraordinary scenario. 'Can you think of a single reason why I should?' she said crisply.

'Because, fundamentally, you're what he always said you were,' said Jennifer. 'You're decent. And because, if he doesn't ride this out, the goalposts will shift, won't they? Old loyalties will be past their sell-by date.'

There was silence while Flora took on board the implication of this. And then she went over to the door and opened it. 'Perhaps you would be kind enough to leave by the back way, too. You obviously know it blindfold.'

Jennifer strolled slowly out of the door. She had a parting shot. 'I'll wait and see which one of you calls me first,' she said.

Flora slammed the door behind her. The phone went, and she was shaking with tension as she picked it up.

'Flora?' Duncan was calling from his office. 'Clive's bloody gone to earth. Have you spoken to him?'

It took Flora a moment to calm down. 'I'll try him,' she said. 'Leave it to me.'

'Someone did this to me, Flora,' Duncan said. Flora gazed implacably out of the window, hardly listening. 'The Leader of the House was just on. I have to make a statement. The PM is keeping his powder dry, to see how I perform.'

'And Sir Donald?' Flora said.

'Not returning my calls. Ian swears the Twenty-two Committee are mustering themselves for an assault from the rear.' Duncan's voice was hoarse with desperation. 'The bastards are going to let me go under, Flora, without even a bloody life raft.'

Flora was calm again. 'You don't need any of them, darling,' she said. 'You've pulled back from the brink before. You can do it again.'

She put down the phone, redialled, and got her father's answering machine assuring her that he would return her call as soon as possible.

Flora waited for the bleep and left a message: 'It's me, Daddy. I feel so wretched about what's happened . . . dragging you into it and . . . do call me when you can. I'm at the flat.'

Flora's optimism had activated Duncan. Before speaking to her he'd felt himself sinking hopelessly into the abyss. Now he could feel the adrenalin coursing through him. He sifted the newspapers on his desk. There must be a way out. At the very bottom of the pile he saw the *Carlingham Chronicle*. His eyes fell on the picture of the demo, the boy with cerebral palsy, and the headline MATLOCK'S MARTYRS.

Something clicked. Duncan banged his desk triumphantly. He took his prepared statement, tore it up and threw it into the waste-paper basket. Pulling a fresh wad of paper towards him, he began scribbling furiously.

An hour later, Duncan walked confidently into the House and took his place on the front bench. The House was packed to the rafters, and there was an atmosphere of suppressed expectancy. As though, Duncan thought dourly, they'd come to watch a Christian being casually chucked to the lions. His colleagues, sombre-faced, shifted up to make room for him, distancing themselves from any contagion.

Duncan was called and there was a *frisson* of excitement in the Opposition benches as he rose and looked slowly around the chamber. 'Madam Speaker. The Press have today raised a number of questions about my integrity which have no factual basis whatsoever and which compel me to speak out in order to set the record straight. Where to start? Did I know about the purchase of Pangbourne Manor by my father-in-law? Yes, of course I did. We're a close-knit family. Naturally we discussed it.' There was a murmur of surprise at this unexpected candour. Duncan, scarcely glancing at his notes, continued in a strong voice. 'Did I know that the sale price was far below its market value? Yes, I knew that also. Did I encourage my father-in-law to use my personal contact with the Chairman of Marlborough Insurance to help influence that price? Yes, in so much as it might influence anything, unequivocally I encouraged it.' Duncan's fellow

Ministers on the front bench were now gazing at him in bewilderment. What was he playing at? Duncan, looking directly at the Opposition, was about to tell them. 'My Right Honourable colleagues on the opposite benches have been busily insinuating that my proposed reform of Child Benefit is based on callousness ... that neither myself, nor this Government, cares about the welfare of children or, indeed, their families –'

'Hear ... hear,' the Opposition shouted eagerly.

'The opposite is true, Madam Speaker ...' Duncan bowed to the Speaker's chair. 'I have, for some time, been concerned about the closure of a local nursery in my constituency ...'

The Opposition brayed in mocking disbelief. The Speaker called crossly for silence.

'... due to ...' Duncan's voice soared above the uproar – '... due to the expiry of their lease and the prohibitive cost of renewing it. This would mean thirty children losing thier nursery places and thirty parents – mostly single mothers – losing their jobs because they'd be obliged to stay at home and look after their children. Having repeatedly tried and failed to get our recently elected Liberal Democrat Council to take up the issue. ...'

The Opposition was now in full cry. Duncan, forced into silence, waited patiently for the hubbub to die down as the Speaker shouted for order.

In Duncan's office, Mark, Ian, Colin, the secretaries and various party workers were perched on every available chair and desk, absorbed by the drama unfolding on the television.

'... to take up this issue,' Duncan was declaiming, 'my father-in-law, knowing of my deep concern, called me to express his personal dismay and his desire to be of construc- tive help. He decided to purchase Pangbourne Manor in order to provide the nursery with a home and so ensure its continued survival.'

The Tory benches were now braying in triumph. They were starting to smell victory and the scent of it was sweet. Madam Speaker was pink-cheeked from shouting 'Order! Order!' over the din.

Colin looked around the room and cried: 'My God, he's going to do it.'

Mark Hollister shook his head in disbelief at Duncan's sheer ability to survive.

Flora lay on the sofa with a glass of champagne in her hand. She was staring at the television in stunned stupefaction as Duncan moved towards the climax of his speech.

'They say actions speak louder than words, Madam Speaker. I hope my own small involvement in this matter demonstrates my continuing concern for the welfare of children and their parents in my constituency. Because it is the self-same concern which governed my thinking over our proposed legislation on Child Benefit. Once the details of that have been made clear to this House, I am confident that . . .' He raised his voice to override the shouts of the Opposition. 'I am confident that those of us who truly care about this issue will see the logic and sense of it. Sadly, there will always be those on the other side of the House who will seek to make cheap political capital out of every scurrilous newspaper headline they read.' Duncan sat down as the House broke into an uproar. The Tories were waving and crowing and shouting their support. The Opposition were yelling back in frustrated rage.

Flora closed her eyes and sagged back against the sofa cushions. And then she pulled the champagne bottle towards her and carefully, meticulously, poured the contents of her glass back into the bottle.

15

The ventilator sighed and sucked, bellowing air into Clive's lungs. The cardiac monitor bleeped and hummed. Flora, sitting by the hospital bed, leant forward and tidied a stray strand of her father's hair. It was as if they had changed places. He, the helpless baby; she, the parent keeping a watchful eye on wires and drips and high-tech life-support systems.

When the phone rang in the flat, she'd been sure it was Duncan, eager with news of his triumph in the House. Instead it was a hospital social worker telling her that her father had suffered a severe stroke.

'We received a call from a Mrs Parfitt – I believe she's your father's cleaning lady – who said that she'd found Mr Woodley sitting in his armchair in front of the television,' the social worker said. 'It seems she thought nothing of it at first, but when she asked Mr Woodley if she could come in and do the Hoovering, she realised there was something wrong and called us. The paramedics did what they could, Mrs Matlock, but I'm afraid he's in a bad way . . .'

'I'll come straight away,' Flora had said. She'd taken a taxi to Euston, caught the next train to Birmingham and picked up another taxi to the hospital. The nurse leading her into the intensive care ward said sympathetically, 'If only they'd got to him sooner, Mrs Matlock. They estimate he'd been there for at least twelve hours.' Drawing aside the curtain, she'd taken Flora's arm and whispered: 'Try not to be upset by the machinery . . . the wires . . . we're doing what we can.'

Clive was lying on the bed, unconscious, a wire taped to the forefinger of one hand, a drip attached to the other arm, as though he were being crucified. Flora had sat there all night, keeping a silent vigil at his bedside. Now, there was an early morning blur of activity in the ward; voices, footsteps, the crackle of starched figures hurrying to and fro with bedpans and breakfast trays.

Flora started talking to her father abstractedly, marshalling her thoughts as she spoke. 'Duncan always said that it was a metabolic thing that made Margaret Thatcher work at such a frantic pace. He said that was her problem. It meant she never slowed down to reflect her actions. He said it was that which made her vulnerable.' She stroked her father's arm rhythmically. 'I think it's the opposite, Daddy. I think if you stop to reflect on what you're doing . . . then you start to doubt your actions . . . and then you're vulnerable.'

Clive lay there impassively. Perhaps it was as well he couldn't hear the self-loathing in his daughter's voice. Flora got a grip on herself and said softly: 'Do you remember the first time I brought Duncan home to meet you? I was dead-heading the daffodils; you and he sat closeted in your study. You barely came up for air, did you? And when we were leaving, you took me aside and patted me on the back and said: "Well done, Flora. Well done." ' Flora stopped, pierced by the poignancy of this memory, and then said: 'You thought I picked him, didn't you? I didn't. He picked me. And you were part of that, Daddy. You were the clincher.' She was piecing together the jigsaw of her thoughts and understanding, for the first time, how simply the pieces slotted into place. 'It was a trade-off. He got his stake in the Shires and the use of your contacts. You got the promise of your name on an Honours list at the end of the line. And me?' Flora's face was a reflection of her father's deathly, blank expression. 'Me . . . I got to spend the rest of my life with the man I love.'

She stayed in the ward a little longer and then, numb with exhaustion, went out into the hospital corridor, sat down on a bench and took out her mobile phone. She'd managed to contact Mrs Lucas earlier, but had been unable to reach Duncan. His secretary answered the phone and said that Mr Matlock still hadn't called in. 'I've left messages all over Westminster for him. Is there any change?'

'No,' Flora said. 'No change.'

She wandered drearily over to a drinks machine, got a cup of coffee, and glanced into the nearby day-room where patients and their relatives were slumped in front of a television, taking minimal interest in a woman politician who appeared to be very angry about something.

Flora recognised Rachel Gold, Duncan's opposite number on the Labour front bench: '. . . and it's not simply the contents of the proposed Bill which is so deeply immoral. It's the fact that Duncan Matlock – with the collusion of the Prime Minister and the entire Cabinet – intended pushing it through the House via the guillotine system. Thus preventing any reasonable time for proper debate . . .'

'Oh, who gives a flying fart,' said a man in pyjamas and dressing-gown. He looked around the room, received a general nod, and switched over to *Emmerdale Farm*.

Flora went back into the corridor as Mrs Lucas and Paul emerged from the lift and came towards her.

'He just insisted on coming, Mrs Matlock,' Mrs Lucas said. 'I told him it was no place for children.'

'It's all right, Mrs Lucas.' Flora crouched down and fussed with Paul's tie. 'There are a lot of wires and machines and things, okay? Don't be frightened.' Paul looked anxious. Flora turned to Mrs Lucas. 'We'll just be a minute.'

Flora and Paul stood, hand in hand, at the end of Clive's

bed. Paul stared at the machinery, overawed. 'Talk to him,' Flora said. 'They say he can hear, even if he can't show it.'

Paul opened his mouth and then closed it again. He felt awkward and foolish. 'Where's Daddy?'

'In London,' said Flora.

Paul said nothing, which Flora realised was a kind of comment in itself. He pointed at a piece of machinery. 'What's that?'

'A ventilator,' Flora said. 'It helps him breathe.'

'What if there's a power cut?' said Paul.

The innocence of the question stabbed Flora like a knife. 'Talk to him, darling. Not to me.'

Paul cleared his throat. 'Hello, Grandad. It's me, Paul.' He looked at his mother. 'What shall I say?'

'Anything, darling. Just so he can hear your voice.'

A man in a white coat came in and gave Flora a significant look. 'Mrs Matlock? Doctor Morgan. Could you spare a minute?'

'Just wait here with grandad, darling,' Flora said to Paul, and followed the doctor into a glass office at the other end of the ward.

Paul waited uncomfortably, watching his mother talking to the doctor and signing some papers. And then she came back, looking strained. She took Paul's hand. 'Say goodbye, darling. They have to see to him now.'

'What did he want?' Paul whispered. 'The doctor?'

'Just say goodbye, darling,' Flora whispered back. 'Please.'

'I'll see you, grandad,' Paul said. 'We'll have a game of chess. Next time I'll let you win. Okay?'

Flora gave him a hug. 'Mrs Lucas is outside in the corridor. Tell her to take you straight home. I'll be back as soon as I can.'

Paul flew out of the ward like a bird released from its cage.

He found Mrs Lucas and the two of them walked along to the lift. It seemed to Paul that it was an age coming, and when it finally arrived and Mrs Lucas stepped in, he remembered something important and swiftly drew back. 'My lucky coin! I was going to give him my lucky coin!'

Before Mrs Lucas could stop him, Paul was speeding back towards the intensive care ward. Clutching his coin, he pulled aside the curtain. The doctor was in there, writing notes. A nurse was taking something out of his grandad's arm, and there was a vicar holding an open Bible. Something else was different. It was a few seconds before Paul registered what it was. The life support equipment was silent, the heart monitor was blank. Paul stared at his grandad's lifeless body. And then he looked over at his mother. Flora was sitting beside the bed, clenched and rigid, staring blankly at the body which had once housed her father's spirit.

Colin Fletcher, Ian Ruby-Smith and Mark Hollister had been hanging around in a corridor in the House of Commons for some time, waiting for Duncan. Eventually, he emerged from an office, laughingly delivering a parting shot. 'Better ship the wanker out to Saudi as ambassador . . . he'd dry out double quick then.' His expression instantly sobered as he closed the door and strode off down the corridor, followed by his retinue. 'What have you got?'

'The rumours were right,' said Ian, 'The bloody 1922 have shoved their oar in.'

'Usual bullshit,' Colin Fletcher said. 'Whether the timing is absolutely right for such sensitive legislation – whether you are the right man now to steer it through.'

'When the hell was all this?' Duncan quickened his pace, closely followed by the others.

'Apparently,' said Ian, 'they had a summit in the Whips' office last night . . .'

'After which the Chief Whip had another with the PM and the Party Chairman at Number 10,' Colin added.

'The word is that the Tory terraces have never been more united in dissent,' said Mark.

'So where does the PM stand on all this?' said Duncan.

'He prefers a retreat to a rout,' Ian replied.

Duncan halted and stared at Ian. 'A public climb-down? Is he mad? The Press will hang our bollocks out to dry.'

'Those we have left,' Colin murmured.

'We have a week to formulate a response,' Mark reminded them.

Duncan thought about this briefly and then set off down the corridor again. 'You know what they say about a week in politics.'

Mark noticed the gleam of survival in Duncan's eye and saw how it enthused the other two with sudden optimism.

'We'll need a few first division players on our team to pull it off,' Ian said.

'More than a few,' said Colin.

'Right.' Duncan stopped and turned to Ian. 'You go round the tea-rooms, Ian. Drop a few well chosen reminders about my stance on the single currency thing. Rub their faces in the dirt if you have to. Report back with a head-count. While you're at it, see what you can pick up on that bloody leak. I want it plugged. ASAP. Colin, you take on Central Office, calm their neuroses. We'll meet back in my office in an hour and see where we're at.'

They started off again and, rounding a corridor, bumped into Duncan's secretary, breathless and anxious. 'Oh, Mr Matlock, there you are. I've been chasing after you all morning. Mrs Matlock rang from the hospital, to say . . . I'm afraid . . . your father-in-law has died.'

Duncan looked at her disbelievingly. 'Clive? Dead?' He stood absolutely still in the corridor, and closed his eyes, momentarily overcome by sadness, even remorse. The men hovered awkwardly around him.

'Oh, well . . . er . . . catch you later,' Ian said.

Flora let herself into her father's house and went straight to the sitting-room. It was just as he had left it. An overturned, half-finished glass of brandy by the chair, a newspaper on the floor, a jacket tossed on the settee. Flora glanced down at the newspaper and saw a headline, MINISTRY OF SCANDAL, beside a picture of Duncan and another of her father.

His absence was tangible. She picked up his jacket and, holding it to her, looked sadly at a framed photograph on the bureau. She and Duncan and her father were standing on the steps of Mindermere House. Her father's face was turned away from her. He was looking at Duncan. There was more than just affection in his face. There was awe.

The phone on the bureau rang, startling her. 'Flora. It's Duncan. Mrs Lucas said I'd find you there. I'm so terribly sorry, love.' Flora couldn't trust herself to speak. 'Are you okay?'

'They said the stroke was so massive, he'd . . .' She swallowed, unable to finish the sentence. 'So I agreed to withdraw the life support.'

'Oh, God,' Duncan said softly. 'Listen, darling, I'm locked into something here. The second I see light, I'll be with you. Sooner if I can. Can you cope until then?'

Flora, still looking at the picture, said dully: 'Yes. Of course I can cope.'

Duncan's mind was racing ahead. 'The funeral. We should liaise. There's people here I'm sure will want to pay their respects. Sir Donald for one. The Party Chairman should get an invite. I'll get Central Office to draw up a list, fax it over.'

'I hoped to make it just family, Duncan,' Flora said.

'Clive would want the full works, wouldn't he? Full pomp and party ceremony. He'd be tickled pink.'

'He loved you, you know,' Flora said. 'Perhaps more than anyone.'

There was a pause on the line before Duncan said. 'Yes. I know. I have to find a way of living with that.' He put down the phone. He was surprised by the truth of his own words.

'How is she?' said Mark. They were in Duncan's inner office.

'You know Flora. Best foot forward.' Duncan suddenly felt tired and distracted; the events of the last two days were starting to devour his energy. He got up and began pacing the room. 'We'd better start with a trawl of his City chums and Lodge members. We can use them for ballast to swell the ranks of mourners.'

'You anticipate much of a turn-out, then?' Mark said.

'If we fine-tune it right. A *coup d'état* is like a revolution, Mark. It's not a question of allies so much as the right arena.'

Mark gave a wry smile. 'And what better venue than the party faithful gathered around the grave of one of their own?'

Duncan turned on him. 'It can have a distorting effect, having one's most callous thoughts mirrored back at one,' he said tersely. 'You'll have to watch that.'

'It's been fucking raining for three days now.' Duncan peered gloomily out of the Ministry car. He was definitely rattled after the meeting with Ian and Colin. Swearing at the weather was something of a release and less dicey than taking it out on Mark – much as he would like to advise his Special Adviser to wipe that cynical sneer off his face.

Ian had reported nil response from his trawl around the House. He had not, however, dared tell Duncan that when he entered the tea-room, Members had either looked through him or concentrated fixedly on their scones and cakes, making him feel like the most unpopular boy in the school. He'd tried nobbling one of the pro-Europeans, who, Ian knew, were desperate for allies, but even he went thumbs down on Duncan. 'Fellow's a total liability – should have been weeded out at the preliminary selection interview.'

Evidently the Press were still snooping around Central Office, and the Party Chairman's secretary had confided in Colin that the general feeling was that Duncan had dragged the party through the mire once too often. Sir Donald Frazier had been unavailable. Nobody knew where to contact him or when he'd be back in his office.

'Look over there, outside the Ministry.' Duncan polished the car window with his sleeve, grabbed Mark's arm and gestured towards a group of rain-sodden protestors, carrying damp placards. 'What do all those damned initials mean?'

'Just guessing now,' said Mark, 'but how about SPA – Single Parents' Association? AAP is probably Action Against Poverty . . .'

'And what the hell's CIC?' Duncan said crossly. 'There are dozens of those.'

'Children In Crisis,' said Mark. 'Whoa, they've spotted us.'

Duncan and Mark got out of the car and were heading towards the main door of the Ministry when a straggle of men and women ran towards them.

'It's him, it's Matlock,' one of the women shouted.

'Mr Matlock. Mr Duncan Matlock, we want a word with you,' a young man shouted.

Duncan stopped and looked at them. 'Oh, God,' he said. 'Smile and say cheese to the nice people.'

'I said it was him,' the first woman said.

Another protestor, who was now close enough to Duncan

to stab a finger into his chest, said: 'We just handed a petition into Number 10. Do you know what it says? It says your White Paper is a crime.'

The rain and their collective anger ignited a spark of outrage, and Duncan could hardly catch what they were saying as they shouted over each other.

'It's no good trying to fob us off with crap about public expenditure and all that baloney.'

'It's creeping privatisation. Just like with the pensions.'

'And the health. The same bloody story all over again.'

'Child Benefit is a lifeline to millions of families, and you want to cut it off.'

As Duncan stepped backwards, he was surrounded by a ring of faces, distorted by anger and excitement. 'Those families who need it will continue to get it,' he said.

'Bollocks they will,' said the young man.

'Why don't you tax the rich instead of robbing the poor?' somebody else screamed, tugging at Duncan's arm. 'You try bringing up three kids on the DSS.'

'The fact is, last year's annual expenditure on State benefits exceeded three billion pounds . . .' Duncan, terrified, was misjudging his audience, giving them the argument he'd used on *World at One* the previous week: '. . . which is higher, in real terms, than any other European country.'

'Stuff the European countries.' An ugly young man pushed his face right up close to Duncan's. 'It's this country we live in.'

The atmosphere was getting more threatening by the second. Mark, who had remained prudently close to the car, opened the door and waved a policeman over from the Ministry steps. Duncan, now pinned against the car, could feel hands tugging at his suit, the hot breath of strangers on his face.

'You're so good at figures. You tell us how much it costs to clothe and feed a child?'

'Yeah. Go on, tell us.'

'The bastard hasn't got a bloody clue.'

The policeman heaved his weight between the protestors and Duncan. 'Okay, let's break it up, shall we? Let the Minister go about his business.'

Duncan dived swiftly into the car after Mark as they heard somebody shout: 'Here's something to help him on his way.' An egg splatted against the window of the car.

Duncan looked out through the slime of raw egg and spoke through clenched teeth. 'I tell you this, Mark. When I find the bastard who leaked that Bill, I'll flush their career down the toilet so fast they won't have time to draw breath.'

16

The day of the funeral was bright and sunny. The great and the good had turned out in force to pay tribute to Clive Woodley. The path up to the church was clogged with large cars disgorging Government Ministers, senior politicians, captains of industry and Conservative party workers. Crowds lined the route, hoping to catch a glimpse of faces they usually only saw on their television screens. An army of reporters and cameramen jostled around the church gate.

Photographers climbed the trees for a better view as the funeral limousines, accompanying the hearse, pulled up outside the church. The funeral march boomed out through the open doors and Duncan, Hugo Patterson and four official pallbearers carried in the coffin, bedecked in blue and white flowers. They were followed by Flora, wan-faced behind her veil, and the two children, each holding their mother's hand, and clutching sodden handkerchiefs. Walking slowly behind them were senior members of the party, including Sir Donald Frazier and Mark Hollister.

Mark edged into a side pew and took stock of the congregation, as Duncan mounted the pulpit. My God, he said to himself, he's managed to muster the lot – Sir Donald, a sprinkling from the Lords, the bit of the front bench that mattered . . . only the PM was missing.

Duncan was speaking, apparently from the heart and without notes. 'We are here today not just to honour a good man, but a very special man. A man who, after a lifetime of successfully running the gauntlet of the City, did not take off to some sun-drenched villa for a well-deserved rest in the autumn of his years, but stayed on in these damp climes to devote himself to the cause which he once told me was the one true love of his life. The Conservative party.'

Is that quite what an only daughter wants to hear at her father's funeral, Mark wondered, as Duncan subtly switched his eulogy to Clive into a party political broadcast. 'And what gives us this confidence? This moral verve? It is the knowledge that our bed-rock, our very spirit, is united, composed of people like my father-in-law.'

Mark saw the heads nodding sagely in dignified agreement. He could only admire the confident way Duncan was seizing the moment and bending it to his advantage. There were tears in the eyes of the local party workers as he said: 'I was proud to call this man "father". I am proud that my children carry his blood in their veins. I am proud to have this chance to say to him, "thank you". Not just for your selfless years of service to the party. Or your financial generosity. Or your unerring wisdom. But for the salutary reminder that true power lies with those who never seek it.' Mark glanced at Ian Ruby-Smith, who was exchanging a discreet smile with Colin Fletcher. 'Last Easter,' Duncan continued, 'Clive stood where I am standing now, to lead us in prayer. He quoted from the Epistle of St Paul. "For we wrestle not against the flesh, and the blood, but against principalities, against powers, against the rulers of darkness of this world, against spiritual wickedness in high places." ' There was a tremor of emotion in his voice as he said: 'Amen, Clive. With the light of your memory to guide us, rest assured we will wrestle on, until the fight is won.'

Someone, momentarily forgetting the venue, broke into applause. The congregation kneeled to pray, and Duncan, now kneeling beside Flora, looked sideways through his fingers, assessing the impact of his words on his audience.

Flora, ghostly behind her veil, watched him doing it, and was dismayed to see people nodding and smiling back. Even a senior Minister mouthed 'good show'.

After the funeral, everyone filtered back to Mindermere House. The hall, living-room and dining-room were packed with mourners drinking champagne and helping themselves to the canapés and midget sandwiches being ferried around by a team of waiters.

Flora noticed Duncan in the centre of a knot of senior politicians, attentive and deferential. Threading her way among the guests, pausing occasionally to receive condolences, she caught the eye of Sir Donald, who was with another group.

Mark appeared at her elbow and said quietly, 'I thought it would all be over by now.'

'I'm afraid we underestimated his resilience,' Flora said.

'Or our own resources.'

Flora, disconcerted by Mark's reply, was about to question him, when Mrs Clegg bore down on her. 'Mrs Clegg. Thank you so much for coming.'

'Your father, he did so much for the party in Carlingham,' Mrs Clegg said. 'I shall miss him. We all will.'

Flora smiled gratefully, and then, dropping her voice, said: 'We should have a little chat, you and I. Can I call you?'

Rosalind Clegg was intrigued. 'I shall look forward to it.'

Mrs Clegg moved on, thrusting her way through the crowd, and Duncan, who appeared to be listening attentively to somebody's rather boring view of the IMF, covertly watched Sir Donald approach Flora. Good girl. She certainly knew how to network.

'Donald,' Flora said. 'How good of you to come.'

'Heavens. The very least I could do,' Sir Donald said. Taking his arm, Flora led Sir Donald out through the french windows, into the garden. They paused for a courteous exchange with the Chancellor of the Exchequer and his entourage, and then ambled down a path banked by manicured flower beds.

'Last time I saw such political *glitterati* was at the opening of the Eurotunnel,' said Sir Donald.

'I was rather hoping it would just be a family affair. As you see, I was overruled.' Flora's stoicism touched Sir Donald, as she knew it would. 'His eulogy was impressive.'

'Very affecting,' Sir Donald agreed. 'But then, Duncan always could cast a spell with his oratory.'

'Because he means what he says. Every word,' said Flora. 'It would be quite fatal to think otherwise.' Sir Donald studied Flora quizzically, as she went on: 'It's like a switch in his brain. He literally discovers the thought as he articulates it. And at that moment he utterly believes it. Even if he knows it to be false. He rides on a crest of adrenalin and total conviction. His audience get swept up along with him.' She allowed a moment for Sir Donald to digest this, and noticed Duncan glancing curiously at them through the sitting-room window. 'But afterwards, he can barely remember what it was he said. Like an actor, shutting down after a performance. All those feelings, that passion, they die with the moment. As if . . .' She trailed off: '. . . as if nothing of value has any real permanence or . . .' She stopped, and looked ruefully at Sir Donald. 'Goodness, you must think me awful saying such things. Much less thinking them.'

'It's a common enough phenomenon in politics these days – the exhilaration of the sound-bite,' Sir Donald said. 'Heroic poses rather lose their currency.'

'That's what I'm afraid of,' Flora said earnestly. 'It's his Achilles' heel, isn't it? He relies so totally on public oratory as a counter-attack. If he was ever robbed of that – I worry he'd have no defences.'

Her words were not lost on Sir Donald, but his answer

was lightly casual. 'Arguably, portable outrage is one definition of charisma.'

'But a base metal, all the same.'

'One which dazzled you.' Sir Donald smiled at Flora.

'I wasn't alone in that, was I?' She looked up at him. 'May I ask you something?'

'Name it.'

'All those headlines. The questions about his integrity. Have they damaged him much?'

'In the long term?'

'Now,' Flora said. 'This Bill. His Ministry.'

'The more sensitive the legislation, the more robust and respected its advocates need to be,' Sir Donald said. 'The two go hand in hand.'

'And charisma is a liability?'

'It's a poor second to statesmanship.' Sir Donald stopped, ostensibly to inspect a rose. 'That's the PM's dilemma, Flora. The Bill was our chance to smash one of the sacred cows of the Welfare State. Its symbolic significance is enormous. If only to finally extinguish the Bevanite torch in Walworth Road.'

'But, Duncan must surely see that?'

'If he did, he'd tender his resignation as Minister for the Family.' Sir Donald shifted his gaze from the rose bed to Flora. 'He'd let us choose a more appropriate person to navigate the Bill through Parliament.'

Flora also inspected the roses. She did not want Sir Donald to see the flash of triumph in her eyes. 'Oh, he can be so obdurate at times.' She sounded genuinely exasperated.

'But, if he *could* be persuaded . . . whoever accomplished that would carry an enormous debt of gratitude.' Sir Donald paused significantly. 'I know for a fact that the PM would express the same sentiment.'

*

Paul was mooching along the landing to his bedroom. Most of the people had left, but he could still hear laughter and chat drifting up the staircase. He couldn't understand why anyone would want to have a party when somebody died. Going into his bedroom, he flung off his funeral suit, the shirt, the tie and the too-tight lace-ups and chucked them on a chair. I bet it wasn't Mum's idea, he said to himself as he put on his old jeans, a sweater and his trainers.

Taking a newspaper cutting from his desk, he settled on the bottom bunk bed and read it through carefully. It was an article he had cut out of the back bit of the *Daily Telegraph*, all about his grandad. The headline read: TRUE BLUE – CLIVE WOODLEY. Paul stared blindly at the flattering picture, which must have been taken when Grandad was a lot younger. Then he noticed the lucky coin on his desk and couldn't help blubbing a bit. He was just going to retrieve the Kleenex box when he saw his father going past the open door. 'Dad . . . ?'

Duncan put his head around the door. 'Not now, old son,' he said. 'We'll have a word later, okay?'

Paul watched his father go into his bedroom, wiped his eyes with a Kleenex, and padded along after him. He opened the door a few inches, enough to see Dad, looking untidy in shirt sleeves, his tie awry, a glass of whisky in one hand and the telephone in the other. He was consulting a list of names as he spoke. 'Well, track him down at his hotel, suggest a breakfast. His brain doesn't get into gear before his noon cocktail. I'll nail him over his kippers.' Dad marked a name on his list and gulped his whisky. 'How did it go with Tim? . . . I didn't get the chance, did I? Every time I tried to nobble him, he darted off like his Y-fronts were on fire.'

Paul tiptoed back to his own room and looked again at the picture in the paper. He wished it was Dad who had died instead of Grandad. And then he felt guilty for even thinking such a terrible thing.

'Come on, darling, bedtime. In you pop.' Flora was folding Joanna's clothes and putting them away and Joanna was sitting on the edge of her bed, swinging her feet, uncharacteristically pensive.

'I've done something awful, Mummy,' she said. Flora glanced at her daughter, surprised. 'Marion Simpson at school? She's a Catholic, and she says there's a place called purgatory, a kind of waiting-room between heaven and hell. She says there's a whole lot of prayers you can say to get people's souls out of there and into heaven . . .' Flora sat down on the bed next to Joanna, waiting for her to continue. 'I meant to say them for Grandad ages ago. Him being so old and everything. I thought God would sort of store them up for him so that when he died he could bypass purgatory altogether.' She looked solemnly at Flora. 'Except I forgot.'

'You can say them now, can't you, darling?' said Flora.

Joanna slipped down onto her knees and adopted a prayerful pose. Then she opened her eyes again. 'What exactly *is* a soul?'

'It's your spiritual part,' said Flora. 'I suppose. The moral part of you . . .' She broke off, gripped by a chill of terror, and clasped Joanna to her. 'When you say them, darling, say one for me, will you? Say one for all of us.'

When Joanna had said her prayers, Flora tucked her into bed, kissed her goodnight and wandered downstairs. Too tired to think, she was mindlessly plumping cushions, emptying ashtrays and stacking glasses on a tray, when Mrs Lucas came in.

'Leave all that, Mrs Matlock, and get off to bed,' she said. 'You must be done in. The catering people have cleared most of it, and I can finish off in a trice.' She took the tray from

Flora. 'It was a lovely service, wasn't it? Just think of it . . . all those famous people coming to say goodbye to Mr Woodley.'

'Thank you, Mrs Lucas,' Flora said. 'Yes, it was a lovely service. And yes, I am a bit done in.'

She went slowly upstairs to bed. All those people, she was thinking dully, summoned to save Duncan Matlock's skin.

He was still hard at work on this project when she went into the bedroom – sprawled on the bed, the whisky bottle at his elbow, the phone wedged under his chin. 'No, he says Shipman's ass is wedged on the fence so tight, we'd have to surgically remove it . . .' Flora was registering every word as she drifted around the bedroom, undressing and hanging up her clothes.

'Oh, he just blanked me out, as predicted. How did Ian do with Toby? Well, tell him to try a Freudian slip. If he confuses inopportune with importune, that should get a result . . . No way, Teddy should be a pushover after that fiasco with his bimbo's expenses in Florida.' Duncan idly watched Flora putting on her nightdress. 'I've got some tedious fête in the afternoon. I'll cry off on compassionate grounds, scoot through my surgery and get back mid-afternoon. We'll have a war cabinet then. Call me if you hear anything. Okay?' He hung up and fell back against the pillows. 'Jesus, it's like wading through treacle.'

'They all came,' Flora said. 'That's a show of solidarity, surely?'

'Clive was a major party funder. Anything less than a full Monty send-off gets the bigwigs clucking their tongues.' Duncan glanced at Flora, getting into bed beside him. 'You're very pallsy with Sir Donald all of a sudden.'

'He was asking me how committed you are to the Bill and the Ministry,' Flora said. 'He didn't say anything specific, and maybe I'm not reading the runes right, but I got the idea he was sounding me out.'

Duncan, who had by now topped up the afternoon champagne with nearly a whole bottle of whisky, stared at her befuddled. 'What?'

'They've something in mind for you, Duncan. Something big.'

'What?' Duncan said again. 'Trade and Industry? The FO? What?'

'He wouldn't say. He just said the PM didn't want a full reshuffle before the summer. That any other Ministerial options open to you would be contingent on your leaving the Ministry for the Family.'

Duncan thought this through carefully. 'Resign, you mean?'

'He said the magnanimity of such a gesture wouldn't go unrewarded. Part of the package, I think he said.'

Her words acted like a charge of adrenalin. Duncan leaped out of bed, grabbed the phone and started pacing up and down the bedroom. 'I'd better call him. Talk to him.'

Flora swiftly followed, taking the telephone from Duncan. 'Sir Donald's using me as his emissary, isn't he? Isn't that how these things work? A word here? A whisper there? So there's no attribution.'

'You think that's why he's been giving me the deep freeze?'

'Has he been?' Flora said innocently. She did wish Duncan would stop pacing up and down.

'I need assurances, don't I? Specifics. They could bury me out in Brussels. In two years no one will even remember my name.'

'Oh, I think they will.'

Flora said this in such a manner that Duncan stopped pacing, sat down heavily on the bed and studied her thoughtfully. His brain was beginning to tick over. 'If I renege on the Bill for a career move, the Right will put an exclusion zone around me – then it's *Belgrano* time. I'll be sitting on the back-benches until the millennium.'

'They seem to be rather deserting you anyway,' said Flora.

Duncan, fuelled by alcohol and despair, turned on her. 'That's what today's bloody exercise was all about, wasn't it? To win the bastards back.'

Flora held her breath and counted slowly to twenty to stop herself saying that actually today's bloody exercise was about burying her father. Instead, she put her arms around Duncan. 'Why don't I talk to Sir Donald for you? Try and get the assurances you need? Then you can make an informed decision.' He looked at her and saw a chink of hope. 'As you say, I do seem to have his ear.'

Duncan kissed the top of Flora's head. 'Jesus, if I just had a few more like you behind me, Flora, I'd be up on that bloody summit by now, instead of clawing up the rock-face on my own.' He climbed into bed and gently pulled her in after him. 'You never mention it, do you, my stupid thing with Jennifer?' Flora turned her face away. 'If it had been the other way around. If it had been you, who . . . I don't know if I could have got back from it. I honestly don't.' He kissed her hand. 'And the sex has never been better, have you noticed? You're like a different woman.' He took her face in his hands. 'God, I love you, Flora. If I didn't have you . . . I . . .' He stopped talking and kissed her. Flora held back. She couldn't deal with his sincerity. 'Hey . . . what is it?'

'Close your eyes,' Flora said. She rolled over so that she was astride Duncan. He looked up. 'Keep them closed,' she said. She was playing a game, acting a role, dispelling genuine emotion. Reaching down, she picked up her stockings, which she'd dropped by the bed, and taking one of his wrists, tied it to the bedhead. 'I'm in control now. Me. Flora.' There was a strange edge to her voice which excited

168

him. She tied up his other wrist. 'Good old Flora. Dear Flora. It's her turn now.'

'Yes, yes,' Duncan whispered. 'Yes, it's your turn, my love. I've waited so long for you to –'

She raised her hand to strike him, and the phone went.

'Shit,' Duncan said. 'Sorry, lovely. Undo us, will you?'

Flora untied one of his wrists to allow him to reach over and pick up the phone. She went into the bathroom and sat on the side of the bath. She could see her disenchanted, dishevelled reflection from every side. She could hear Duncan in the bedroom. 'What did he say? Yeah, but will he go on record? You know what a bloody wet he is . . . Tomorrow, then.' The phone clicked. 'Oh, Flora? Flora, love?'

Drearily, she went back into the bedroom.

Suzie and Margot were standing just inside the door of the Civic Centre as Flora and Duncan arrived for his surgery. 'Good to see you again,' Duncan said, striding past them. 'Flora?'

Flora, who had stopped to have an encouraging word with the two women, hurried after Duncan and sat down next to him at the large table in the centre of the room. A party worker was already there, notebook and clipboard at the ready.

'Those women from the day nursery,' Duncan said. 'What number are they?'

The party worker consulted her clipboard. 'Number six.'

'And how many will we get through today?'

'About twenty-five?'

'Make them twenty-six,' Duncan said.

The party worker made a note and Duncan murmured quietly to Flora. 'Ring up Roger Graveley when you get home. Tell him there's no rush processing Clive's will. If we procrastinate long enough, this whole absurd nursery thing will go down the tubes. Pangbourne Manor will revert to you with the rest of the estate.' He smiled around the room. 'Okay, ladies, on we go.' He adjusted his notes on the table and patted Flora's hand. 'It's all about seeing a window of opportunity and going for it. Name of the game, my love.'

Duncan left for London and his war cabinet straight after the surgery, and Flora put on her straw hat and went to the garden fête. She was just making her way through the crowds, with the Mayor and other civic dignitaries, when she had the good fortune to spot Rosalind Clegg, resplendent in a floral coat and hat, at the bring and buy stall.

Extricating herself from the official group, she went across to join her. 'Mrs Clegg, how timely. I was going to call you this evening. I'm afraid I only have a minute, I've a marrow competition to judge. Will you walk with me?'

'By all means.' Mrs Clegg fell into step beside Flora, who took her arm.

'I badly need your advice, Rosalind,' she said with concerned sincerity. 'You remember, in the House last week, Duncan said he had made repeated efforts to get the local Council to take action on the nursery closure?' Rosalind nodded, waiting for Flora to reveal what was on her mind. 'Well, he didn't. Not once. Either personally or in his capacity as an MP. It's only a matter of time before the Liberal Democrat Councillors realise the political potential of such a *faux pas* and call the Press, isn't it? I just can't believe he's been such a fool. And I shudder to think what the local party will do when they hear about it. I just don't know what on earth we can do.'

Rosalind Clegg gazed for quite a long time at the coconut shy. Then she said: 'Your husband must remedy the situation. And quickly.'

'You think it can be remedied?' Flora asked innocently.

'If he makes a public apology to the House for misleading them, it is possible that would assuage the criticism. But he must act soon. Before the party is afflicted with yet more lurid headlines about his integrity.'

'And if he declines to apologise?'

'It'll be political kamikaze if he doesn't,' said Mrs Clegg firmly. 'It will be my duty, as vice chairman, to put up a motion demanding his resignation at the next Association meeting. I would have no choice.' Touched by Flora's troubled expression, she pressed her hand reassuringly. 'I'm sure it won't come to that. Not once the gravity of the situation is explained to him.' They had reached the garden produce tent and Rosalind Clegg gestured towards the vegetables. 'Your marrows are waiting.'

Flora desperately wished that she didn't have to take Paul back to school. As they were driving up to the entrance, she slowed down and said, 'You really, really want to go on boarding?' Paul nodded. 'I'm sorry it's been such a beastly half-term, darling.' Flora took his hand. 'Grandad and everything . . . and Dad and I have been so busy . . .' She reached into the back seat for Paul's case. 'Do you want me to come in with you?' Paul shook his head. They both got out and Flora embraced him. 'You will call me, darling. Tell me how you're doing?'

Paul nodded again. Flora watched sadly as he trudged towards the door. She was just about to get back into the car when Richard Pearson appeared.

'Mrs Matlock?' He looked a trifle awkward. 'I was hoping to catch you. Listen . . . I'm afraid Paul's boarding . . . it's not working out quite as we'd hoped. It suits some boys better than others, of course, but he's a solitary lad, you see. The others mistake that for arrogance. They gang up on him and – I'm afraid his father being so much in the public eye – it does give them ammunition.'

Flora, agonised by the housemaster's words, said: 'He won't come home. I asked him again just now. He's adamant.' Mr Pearson shifted from foot to foot, embarrassed by her candour. 'But he will,' Flora said in a firmer tone of voice. 'Soon he'll have no reason not to come home.' She looked straight at Mr Pearson. 'Take care of him for me until then, will you?'

The following evening, Flora climbed the elegant staircase of the Athenaeum Club, another male bastion, passing heavy, gilt-framed portraits of long-dead, wigged Ministers and Peers of the Realm. At the top of the staircase, Sir Donald was waiting for her, beaming a welcome.

'I hope I'm not keeping you from anything,' Flora said.

'Only a tedious reception for some cultural delegation from Eastern Europe at Number 10 . . .' Sir Donald took her arm, opened a huge ornate door and ushered her into one of the clubrooms: '. . . which rather begs the question that they actually *have* a culture.'

Flora was aware of a lot of mahogany and leather, the rustle of newspapers and a veil of cigar smoke. A waiter was circling the room with a drinks trolley. They sat down by a roaring log fire.

No wonder men prefer going to their clubs to going home to their wives, Flora thought, accepting a Scotch from the waiter. 'So, still no women members?' she said.

'Thank God.' Sir Donald grinned at her. 'Or before we knew it the place would be stuffed with pot-pourri and antimacassars.'

Flora smiled. The fire crackled and hissed. She sipped her drink. There was a small, companionable silence before she said: 'I hope you're not one of those who kill the messenger,

Donald.' He glanced at her. 'He just won't hear of resigning. I tried, but . . .'

Sir Donald concealed a small flash of anger. 'I'm sure you did. That's in no doubt, my dear.'

'He said something . . .' Flora began tentatively. 'Something about . . . now what was it? Something about "not without the right inducements". He wants another Ministry. And not just any Ministry. He wants to choose it.'

Sir Donald was no longer able to hide his anger. 'The man is hardly in a position to barter.'

'I know,' Flora said. 'We had the most fearful to-do about it.' She looked helplessly at Sir Donald. 'I just couldn't reach him.'

'His attitude is going to be a great disappointment to a lot of people,' Sir Donald said.

Flora looked concerned. 'Yes, I appreciate that.'

Sir Donald gazed pensively into the fire. 'He must be extraordinarily sure of his support, to make such a bid.'

'That's the part I don't understand,' Flora said. 'His support is diminishing almost daily, isn't it?'

'Hourly, from what I hear.'

'Perhaps he has a secret weapon we don't know about.'

Sir Donald pondered this. 'If he's forced to resign, he'd be entitled to his day in court, wouldn't he? To speak out in the House. Presumably he thinks the PM would want to avoid the embarrassment of that, at whatever cost.'

'Oh, no.' Flora appeared totally shocked by this idea. 'I can't believe he would ever contemplate such a disloyal –'

'Either that, or his imperative is sheer arrogance. Neither one much commends him.' Sir Donald immediately regretted such bluntness. 'That was tactless. I apologise.'

Flora shrugged, as if she had too many other things to worry about. Sipping her drink, she said: 'Mind you, I think what he's most worried about is the possibility of his Child

Benefit thing going in front of a Select Committee. Like they did over the pit closures? It diffused all the outrage, didn't it? Gave everyone time to recoup and regroup?' She gave Sir Donald time to digest this and then said: 'But Duncan just hates Select Committees. All those tedious questions and cross-examinations. He says it's like putting your whole political career on the line.'

'Not to mention robbing him of the chance to use his oratory skills,' said Sir Donald thoughtfully.

'Exactly.' There was another silence before Flora said, 'I'm sorry. I haven't been much help, have I?'

'On the contrary,' Sir Donald said truthfully. 'I find all our conversations most enlightening.'

They finished their drinks and Flora followed Sir Donald's lead as he stood up. He folded her hands in his, a prelude to farewell. Flora clasped his hands, and speaking shyly, as if she were anxious about his reaction, said: 'I keep telling myself . . . what's good for the party is good for Duncan. That confiding in you isn't disloyalty, but . . .'

'I consider it a great compliment, my dear. And I assure you I won't abuse it.' Sir Donald pressed Flora's hands and found himself gazing deeply into her eyes. He was disconcerted by the spark of mutual attraction he saw there. Looking away quickly, he summoned the waiter. 'Tell my driver I'm going back to Number 10.'

Flora watched him go, and then opened her bag, took out her phone and Filofax and dialled a number. 'Jennifer Caird? That matter we talked about. The lifting of your blockade in Westminster. I'm prepared to talk about it now, if you are.'

At the other end of the phone, Jennifer said: 'He's losing the fight, isn't he?'

'It seems so, yes.'

'I wonder which is the hardest.' Jennifer's voice was softly sympathetic. 'Losing, or the fear of it?'

Flora, who had no intention of entering into a caring discussion about Duncan's feelings, said: 'I'm on my way back to Mindermere and the children. I wondered, it's so difficult for me to keep dragging down to London, could you possibly come up to Carlingham? There's a very good hotel – The Swan. I could book you a room. Say, Friday night?' She couldn't resist adding: 'They have four-poster beds and jacuzzis. You'll love it.'

She cut off the call and redialled. 'Mr Montford? I have some information which may be of interest . . .'

Flora found Duncan back at the flat, edgy and preoccupied, surrounded by a debris of newspapers and Ministry papers.

He jumped up as she came through the door. 'What did he say?'

Flora tugged off her coat. 'It's Trade and Industry.'

'Definitely?'

'Definitely. But he said if you try to get confirmation, they'll deny it. To a man.'

'Did he give you any idea of the time-frame?'

'He says there's a possibility of the Bill going in front of a Select Committee first.'

'Oh, Jesus.' Duncan sank down onto a chair.

'Just to give the PM time to stage-manage things,' Flora said. 'Let the media dust settle. Appease the wets. All that.'

Duncan ran his fingers through his hair distractedly. 'If it goes in front of the Home Affairs Committee they'll roast me.'

'By the time they report, you'll be heading for the DTI, won't you? *Après moi*, etc?' Duncan seemed unconvinced. Flora seated herself on the arm of his chair and put a consoling arm round his shoulders. 'There'll be other Bills, darling. Trade and Industry. It's a quantum leap. Next stop, the Exchequer?'

'I don't know, Flora.' Duncan shook his head. 'There's a distinct whiff about all this.'

'He said the House was like a tinder-box. The Whips are ducking and diving like prize-fighters. Anything's better than an enforced resignation, isn't it?' Duncan continued to look uneasy. 'Well,' Flora said, 'I'm going to take a shower. It's been quite a day, one way and another.'

In the bathroom, Flora switched on the shower, sat down on the closed lavatory seat and dialled Rosalind Clegg's number. 'Mrs Clegg? Flora Matlock. I spoke to Duncan about that matter. He absolutely refuses to apologise to the House. I just couldn't reach him, I'm afraid.' She looked into the mirror, and was momentarily repelled by the face of the woman reflected there.

'Did you warn him of the consequences?' Mrs Clegg said. 'My motion, and – ?'

'Oh, I did, yes, but . . .' Flora turned away from the mirror. 'He said it would take more than the menopausal moral right to oust him. That no one would ever take you seriously.' There was a splutter of rage at the other end of the phone. 'Rosalind? I want you to feel absolutely free to act in the best interests of the party. Don't worry about me in all this.'

Flora pushed the aerial into the phone, switched off the shower. Then she raised the lid of the lavatory and flushed the toilet. She remained standing there for some time, thoughtfully watching the water cascade down the bowl.

17

Mrs Lucas was Hoovering the sitting-room to a repeat of *Just a Minute*. Switching off the Hoover so she could listen to Paul Merton, who always made her laugh, she was irritated to discover that her programme was over and the news had started.

'. . . announced today that his controversial legislation on Child Benefit will be the subject of an enquiry by the Home Affairs Select Committee. Duncan Matlock had this to say . . .' Mrs Lucas, who had been about to turn off the radio, turned it up louder, and Duncan's voice resonated around his own sitting-room. 'I am delighted with this development as it gives all the interested parties a chance to voice their opinions on my proposed Bill.'

Out in the garden, Flora was pruning dead branches with unaccustomed gusto. She waved her secateurs at Mrs Lucas and came up to the window. 'I've got to go into Carlingham in half an hour, Mrs Lucas. Do we need anything?'

'We're nearly out of Duraglit,' Mrs Lucas said, 'but we're all right for dinner. I don't suppose Mr Matlock will be back?'

'Not for a day or two,' Flora said. 'He's got a lot on in London.'

'That's what I thought,' said Mrs Lucas. 'I just heard on the radio that he'd got to talk to some sort of Select Committee.' Flora raised an eyebrow. 'He sounded very pleased about it.'

Flora's brief surge of sympathy evaporated as she caught

sight of the Orangery. 'Oh, another thing, Mrs Lucas,' she said. 'Joanna won't be home tomorrow evening, she's spending the weekend with a schoolfriend. If you want to take yourself off for a break?'

'Why, thank you, Mrs Matlock,' Mrs Lucas said. 'I might just do that.'

The Radbourne Day Nursery was situated in the down-at-heel end of town, right behind the run-down High Street, which had died when they built the new out-of-town shopping centre.

Flora parked her car on a waste lot and went in. The interior of the nursery was as desolate as the exterior. A few children's paintings still clung to the walls, most of the scaled-down chairs and tables were stacked in a corner, and there were bits of equipment spilling out of packing cases. Flora, picking up a discarded doll with a missing leg, was struck by the poignancy of the place; as if the spirit of the children somehow lived on.

Hearing footsteps, she turned to see Margot and Suzie coming into the room.

'Why, Mrs Matlock!' Suzie put two mugs of steaming coffee and a packet of biscuits down on a tiny table and drew up three baby chairs. They sat around the table as if they were about to join in a children's tea party.

Flora looked around the room. 'It hadn't sunk in before – the awful waste.' Neither of the two women replied. They were tired and dirty from packing up the nursery, but their fatigue seemed to Flora to be more than just physical. 'I hope you know I've always tried to be your ally in all this,' she said.

'Of course we know,' said Suzie.

Flora rose and went over to the window. She looked out at the garden, which had been converted into a playground with battered climbing-frames, toys and a small, overgrown flower bed. 'Is that it?' she said. 'The garden where the children picked those wild flowers for me?' Margot and Suzie seemed puzzled. 'You gave them to me, remember? Just after the story broke about my husband's affair with that woman?' She realised that they were both slightly taken aback by her frankness. It was as though she were chatting to two old friends as she said, 'I see pictures of myself sometimes. Taken before that. And others, taken afterwards. I marvel how I can look the same. Yet nothing is the same.' Suzie exchanged a worried glance with Margot and then they both stared at Flora. They just couldn't fathom what all this was leading up to. 'I see now that empowerment is about being part of something. For men like my husband, it is being part of a political party . . . the alchemy of intrigue and ambition and . . .' Flora stopped, as if the thought was too difficult to articulate, and returned to sit on the small chair. 'There's something I have to tell you,' she said. 'My late father never made any request, legal or personal, that Pangbourne Manor should be turned over to you for your nursery.'

'But, your husband said –' Margot began.

'He said it in the House of Commons,' Suzie looked at Flora accusingly.

Flora shrugged helplessly, as if Duncan's utterances were beyond her comprehension. She tugged some papers from her handbag and laid them on the table. 'The details of my father's Will. As you see, there's no mention of it. The house becomes mine, as part of his overall estate.'

Margot took the papers, scanned them and passed them to Suzie. 'So that's that.'

Suzie looked at the Will. 'I knew it was too good to be true.'

Flora waited a minute before she said: 'We could make it true. Once the probate is officially settled, I could sign the house over to you.' They gazed at her incredulously. 'No conditions,' Flora said. 'You would have complete autonomy.'

The two women shifted uneasily. Suzie was the first to speak. 'I don't know what to say.'

'How can we ever repay you?' said Margot.

Flora fiddled with the discarded doll. Eventually she said, with restrained emotion: 'Lies should always be exposed, don't you think? By whoever encounters them, regardless of political persuasion?'

'Listen,' Margot said, 'it's all we can do to get through the day.'

'How I know that feeling.' Flora got up abruptly and turned her back, as though she didn't want them to see her battling for self-control. 'He cares no more about his own children than he does about yours,' she said bitterly. 'They're all hostages to his fortune. Just as I am. That's what makes it all so terribly hard, you see. I've tried to talk to him, of course I have. Reason with him . . .' Her voice wavered with emotion, and the two women were now embarrassed and concerned – '. . . but I just can't reach him. You must think me very weak and foolish.'

'Not at all.' Margot reached for the papers. She was beginning to get an inkling of Flora's agenda. 'The thing about exposing lies – I mean politicians' lies – is that nobody cares. They don't give a toss.'

'What is it they say?' Flora looked directly at Margot. 'Don't care was made to care?'

The women exchanged another look. Margot held up the Will. 'Can we keep this?' Flora nodded.

'Where shall we say we got it?' said Suzie.

'An anonymous source?' said Margot.

educational vouchers ('My aim is to give every parent the right to choose the school they want for their child . . .') and was beginning to relax, when Bill Bingham, whom Duncan had always considered a harmless old buffer from his own back-benches, raised the provocative Single Mother issue. 'The single parent associations have told us that they consider this so-called cash incentive to single mothers discriminatory and derisory,' he said. 'What puzzles me is why you never sought their views when you were drawing up the Bill?'

'I'm very glad you raised that point . . .' While Duncan quoted figures about the uneconomic cost of nation-wide nursery care, he was wondering why nobody from Smith Square had thought to put a muzzle on old Bill Bingham.

And then, some woman he'd never seen before, the only Lib Dem on the Committee, started getting personal. 'In the light of your own extra-marital affair, Minister, it does rather pose the question as to whether you are qualified to speak about family issues at all.'

'My personal life has no bearing on this matter whatso-ever,' Duncan replied, in what he considered to be a dignified and restrained tone.

He had need for further restraint when Bill Bingham leaned forward again, and said in a deceptively mild manner: 'You don't think, then, that perhaps the quite extraordinary hostility the public feels about your proposals is linked with the recent publicity about your personal life?'

Eventually the chairman said how much they had all appreciated Duncan's frankness and would like to thank other concerned parties him for giving his time. 'We will, of course, be talking to other concerned parties, and will be issuing our report as soon as possible.'

Duncan, dismissed, went out into the corridor, leaned against the wall, closed his eyes, and breathed calmly and deeply. Every Saturday evening the Beeb beamed gems from Select Committee meetings to the nation. He just hoped to God this wouldn't be one of them.

He opened his eyes abruptly as he heard an irate voice shouting: 'Child Benefit is one of the mainstays of income for a single parent family . . .'

Just above Duncan's head was a closed-circuit television relaying the proceedings from the chamber. An Opposition back-bencher was getting up now: 'And when, Madam Speaker, does the Right Honourable gentleman intend apologising to the House for deliberately misleading . . .'

Duncan walked speedily along the corridor towards the exit. He could hear Rachel Gold, his regular sparring partner, calling out derisively: 'What's next – taxing disability pensions?' And the Lib Dem spokesman saying: 'To cheat the most needy in our society is not just cynical and callous . . .'

Duncan quickened his pace and went out of St Stephen's Gate towards Whitehall.

Ian, Colin and Mark were watching the midday news in the Ministry for the Family office, and the mood was sombre.

'They've got that bolshie bloke from the NUT on now,' Ian said

'. . . We in the NUT object to the idea that the state education sector is to be yet further demoralised by the introduction of education vouchers to the private sector . . .'

'And his chief henchman,' said Colin.

'. . . The Tory wolf – in the guise of Duncan Matlock – is sniffing at the door of Child Benefit *and* state education . . .'

'So, he's managed to alienate the teachers as well as the single mothers,' said Mark. He looked at the other two. 'Who next? More important, what now?'

'How about Jeremy?' Colin said.

Ian shook his head. 'Saw him last night at the Carlton. Very anti, I'm afraid. He said something about Duncan offending his wife, not turning up at one of her charity do's.'

Mark smiled. 'He always uses her as an opt-out. It's rats and sinking ships, isn't it?'

'Sometimes,' Colin said, 'I think there's a lot to be said for the "one bonk and you're out" rule.'

'It would certainly simplify matters,' said Ian, who hadn't managed to get home before 10 p.m. for the past two weeks.

They broke off, and started fiddling with papers as Duncan came through the door. There was an air of desperation about him as he charged through to his inner office and gestured for them to follow.

'Well?' Mark said.

'Anything but bloody well,' Duncan replied. 'I swear somebody at Smith Square stitched me up.'

He looked at his team. They were looking back at him with a sort of pity. As if, he thought, I had something terminal.

Flora was in the kitchen making scones, efficiently whirring dough with her Magimix. Every now and again she stopped and glanced at the portable television on the dresser. She was tuned into the local news, where Margot and Suzie could be seen outside the abandoned nursery, brandishing Flora's legal papers at a group of reporters and curious spectators.

'We know for a fact that Duncan Matlock lied when he said his father-in-law bought that house for our nursery,' Margot was saying.

'He only pretends to care for children.' Suzie raised her voice above the excitement of the onlookers. 'The thirty children who lost their nursery places mean nothing to him.'

Flora gave her Magimix another whirr. Rosalind Clegg was now self-importantly filling the screen. She was standing on the steps of the Carlingham Conservative headquarters, reading out a statement. 'Duncan Matlock's recent actions have caused the Association increasing concern. We feel we have no choice but to voice this concern through a motion of no confidence.'

Flora scooped the scone dough out of her mixer and switched off the television. Everything seemed to be turning out according to her recipe.

'Double Scotch,' Duncan snapped at the waiter. He watched, with increasing irritation, as the young man, little finger daintily crooked, poured out the drink. 'Another bloody left-hander,' he said to Mark as the waiter withdrew. 'These places are clogged with them.'

Mark gazed resolutely into the fire, without replying. Duncan had insisted on them both coming to the Athenaeum to nobble Sir Donald who, sources had revealed to Ian, was dining at the club. They had been sitting in the clubroom for at least an hour already.

Duncan looked impatiently at his watch and then around the room at the members contentedly dozing, reading the evening papers or sharing pre-dinner drinks. 'Do you know how long I've been waiting for my membership here? Three bloody years. You can't get in for love or money. Unless it's old money, of course. That's still where the power lies.'

Mark had noticed that Duncan's thoughts were becoming increasingly unconnected and abstracted, which he put down to pressure topped up with alcohol. 'Not for much longer,' he said.

'What do you mean?' Duncan looked at him suspiciously; he'd taken to looking at everybody suspiciously recently.

'Information superhighway will be where it's at,' Mark said. 'Shopping via computer. Your TV screen will let you amble around an entire shopping mall and make your purchases without ever straying from the comfort of your home.'

Duncan couldn't imagine what Mark was blathering about. He looked at his watch again. If only he could get hold of Donald. Explain, get his advice.

'They'll hold referendums the same way,' Mark was saying. 'From Strasbourg to the Senate. Virtual reality giving power to the people.'

'Then God help all of us,' Duncan said bluntly.

He looked up expectantly as the waiter came over. 'I'm afraid Sir Donald is dining with guests, Mr Matlock. He can't be disturbed.'

'So, we'll wait until he's finished dining,' Duncan said, sinking back in his armchair.

'I'm afraid this room is designated for members' guests only, sir,' the waiter said.

Duncan stared at the waiter frostily and held out his glass. 'Bollocks to that.'

The waiter hesitated and then, taking the glass, refilled it and passed it to Duncan.

Mark rose. 'I won't be a minute,' he said, and strolled off towards the Gentlemen's toilet.

Flora was sitting at Duncan's study desk, sipping a glass of wine. The phone went and she answered it instantly. 'Yes?'

It was the call she had been waiting for. Mark Hollister was at the other end of the line. 'I'm calling you from the Athenaeum,' he said. 'Sir Donald is eating in the dining-room and Duncan is simmering in the clubroom. We're about ready for your finale.'

Flora put down the phone. Deliberately not giving herself time to question her motives or the consequences of what she was about to do, she picked it up again and dialled the Athenaeum.

'Sir Donald Frazier, please. I understand he's dining in your restaurant.'

Sir Donald was put on the line. 'Hello?' he said uncertainly.

'Donald? It's me – Flora.' She suppressed a sob. 'I'm at my wits' end, Donald. I really am.'

Donald heard the anguish in her voice. 'Where are you?' he said. 'I'll come to you.'

'No, no, I'm at home, I . . .' Flora halted, as if in despair. 'Oh, this is ridiculous. I can't burden you with my . . . I'll call back when I'm . . .'

'Flora, wait,' Sir Donald said urgently. 'Calm down, now. Tell me what's happened.'

'You remember when we last met? I was so afraid you'd think me disloyal. That's the awful irony of it all.' She was toying idly with Duncan's American Express card as she was speaking. 'He's seeing Jennifer Caird again. Right here, in Carlingham. She's booked in at the Swan Hotel tonight.'

'I can't believe he'd be such a damned idiot,' Sir Donald said.

'I couldn't either,' Flora said. 'I got someone to check it. The room was booked on his credit card.' Sir Donald gripped the receiver as the poor girl's voice splintered with emotion. 'I just don't know which way to turn. What to do.'

He thought for a moment and then said: 'I want you to be very clear on how you answer this, Flora. In choosing to confide in me, am I right in assuming you expect me to act on this information?'

He heard Flora gasp and draw in her breath. 'Oh no . . . no. I rang you as a friend. Because I think of you as my friend.'

'Please believe me when I tell you that whatever action I do take will also be governed by friendship,' said Sir Donald.

He searched for the right encouraging words. 'Give yourself a hug, my dear. Try to sleep.'

On his way back to his table he was stopped by the young waiter he'd spoken to earlier. 'Mr Matlock is still waiting, Sir Donald. Shall I tell him you've left?'

'Yes.' Donald had made up his mind. 'And tell him I'm spending the weekend at Chequers. I can't be reached.'

At Mindermere House, Flora hung up the phone and put Duncan's American Express card back in the top drawer of the desk. It won't be long now, she said to herself. She slowly finished her wine and went upstairs to get undressed.

She returned to the study shortly, wearing her favourite white silk dressing-gown. Taking twigs and logs and fire-lighters from the log basket, she laid them meticulously in the grate. She put a light to them, and then knelt back and smiled, satisfied with her handiwork.

'Fancy another?' Duncan was searingly aware that he wasn't going to get back-up from Donald Frazier, or anyone else, for that matter. He was scared of sobering up to the reality of his situation.

'Not for me,' said Mark. 'I'm afraid I've got a dinner date.'

'I'm not going to let the bastards get away with this.' Duncan's voice was slurred and he had some difficulty getting suavely out of the armchair. 'There must be some way we can nail all these damned lies and innuendoes.'

'Best thing you can do is get some rest,' Mark said. 'Your driver's outside. I'll tell him to take you back to the flat.'

Outside, Mark helped Duncan into his car. 'I'll pick up the first editions on my way home,' he said. 'If there's anything of interest I'll drop by later.'

Duncan let himself into the flat, chucked his coat and his case onto a chair and looked around for a bottle of Scotch and the telephone. The phone went before he located the whisky.

'Duncan? Martin Pryce here.' Duncan smiled gratefully into the phone. Good old Martin. A friend in need is a friend . . . But Martin's call was far from friendly.

'I don't know what the hell you're playing at, Duncan,' he said, 'but I do know that you've besmirched the good name of my company, the board has gone off its collective rocker, and if it hadn't been for some pretty fast footwork on my part I'd be out of a job.'

'But –'

'I had no intention of selling that bloody house, anyway.' Martin ignored Duncan's interruption. 'It was only as a favour to Flora that Peggy and I –'

'No,' Duncan said. 'Not Flora, it was Clive, you've got it wrong there, old chap. It was Clive who –'

'If I were you, I'd lay off the booze,' Martin said sharply. There was a click on the phone. Duncan listened to the silence for a while and then realised that Martin had hung up.

'You've got it all wrong, Martin,' he murmured. He gazed reflectively at the phone. Who else was there? There must be somebody he could trust, a staunch ally who had always stood four-square behind him? He dialled Hugo Patterson's number. Surely, Hugo couldn't willingly have endorsed Rosalind Clegg's disloyal statement?

Hugo, disturbed in the middle of his dinner, was circumspect. He waffled on about his deepest regrets . . . taking into account how many years they had worked together for the common cause . . . Duncan must understand his position as chairman of the Carlingham Conservative party . . . too many lies . . . Pangbourne Manor . . . local day nursery . . . he'd had the feelers out . . . voters wouldn't wear it . . .

What it all boiled down to, Duncan realised wearily, was that Hugo Patterson also wanted him out.

He put down the phone, found the whisky, swallowed a long, deep drink and fell back onto the sofa.

Suddenly, he was startled awake by the sound of the entry buzzer. Groggy with sleep and alcohol, he stumbled over and pressed the entry button. Mark Hollister announced himself over the intercom. Duncan looked blearily at the clock. Christ, it was past midnight.

Mark walked in with an armload of newspapers. 'Brace yourself.' He dumped the papers in Duncan's arms and followed him over to the sofa. 'Not even a bloody warning shot over our bows.'

Duncan collapsed onto the sofa and gazed in dumb astonishment at the front page of one of the tabloids. The headline read: HE'S STILL AT IT! There was a photograph of a four-poster bed and the caption, MATLOCK'S LOCAL LOVE NEST. 'What?' Duncan picked up another paper, showing Jennifer Caird alighting from a taxi in front of a hotel – surely the Swan in Carlingham? This one was headlined: MINISTER OF THE FAMILY DUMPS ON HIS FAMILY AGAIN! 'How?' Duncan looked up at Mark in stunned disbelief. 'I didn't . . . I don't understand?'

Mark looked back at him impassively and shrugged his shoulders.

Duncan bundled all the newspapers together, grabbed his overnight bag, stuffed it indiscriminately with the official papers littering the coffee table, and slung his jacket over his shoulders.

He pushed a hand through his dishevelled hair. 'I've got to get home,' he said. 'To Flora.'

Mark gave the chaotic flat a cursory glance and closed the door behind them. There was a merciless glint of humour behind his opaque glasses as he envisaged the upcoming newspaper-headline. 'It has just been announced that the Minister for the Family has resigned to spend more time with his family.'

Duncan's driver dropped him outside Mindermere House. He pushed open the front door. 'Flora?' He could see a chink of light through the open study door. 'Flora?' There were no lights on in the room, but she was sitting on the floor, in front of a glowing fire, wearing something white and silky. Duncan found the scene hearteningly consoling.

'Did Mark call you?' He dumped the newspapers on the floor beside Flora, and tugged off his coat. Flora nodded and glanced at the headlines in the papers without speaking. Duncan fixed himself a drink, brought back the bottle and dropped down onto the floor beside her.

Putting a hand under her chin, forcing her to look into his eyes, he said: 'It's lies, Flora. All lies. I've not set eyes on her in all this time. I swear it. That's the God's honest truth.'

'I know it is,' Flora said simply.

Duncan loosened his tie, pulled at his drink. He felt wrecked; his thoughts were too scattered to take in what she had just said.

'They phoned from Chequers,' Flora said. 'They want you to call back in the morning.'

'I'm finished, Flora.' He looked at her in the haze of firelight. She had never looked more hauntingly beautiful. 'Someone did this to me. It was premeditated and calculated. All of it. Right from the start. A systematic destruction of my credibility and my career.' He finished the drink and poured another. Flora sat watching him. 'Think about it,' Duncan said vehemently. 'The leaking of the Bill? That débâcle with Clive and that bloody nursery? That Clegg woman and her machinations? Every ally I've ever had, turned against me.

To be the object of so much hate. And why? What the hell did I do to deserve it?'

He looked into her eyes, glinting in the firelight. 'You're the one I don't deserve.' He pulled her to him. 'You alone kept the faith. Only you.' He started kissing her. He had never felt such intense love for her. He put his head on her bare breasts and she held him to her, as though he were a child. 'Tell me you love me, Flora. I need to hear it. Now. This minute.'

Flora caressed his head, her eyes full of unshed tears. 'I'll always love you, Duncan.'

He pulled her to the floor, started tugging off his shirt. Flora stared at him and, as he lowered himself on to her, she turned away.

'No,' Duncan said fiercely. 'No games this time. To hell with fucking games.'

They started to make love, tenderly, with genuine, mutual emotion. It was an equal partnership, and for both of them it was too late. Afterwards, they lay nakedly entwined, dozing in front of the fire.

After a while Flora roused, pulled her robe around her, and sat for a while, gazing into the fire. Then she went quietly out of the room.

Duncan woke up to find Flora standing over him. He looked at her and blinked, bleary with sleep. She was wearing Jennifer Caird's black silk underwear.

'We made love here that weekend, didn't we?' she said quietly. 'The weekend before you told me about Jennifer Caird.' Duncan stared at the cami-knickers and at the strange, flat resignation in Flora's face. 'Rather suits me, don't you think?' she said. 'What was it you said? If you see a window of opportunity – go for it?'

Duncan felt as though he had been winded, as though the

air had been sucked out of his lungs. 'My God. It was you.' The realisation stabbed him like a physical pain.

'You're wrong, Duncan,' Flora said. 'It's not about hate. Quite the reverse in fact.'

He stared at her, trying to fathom her meaning. And then he stood up. 'Take that shit off.'

'Why?' Flora said. 'I thought you liked it.'

'You look like a fucking tart,' Duncan said. 'Take it off.'

Flora remained standing there, smiling. Her smile detonated a terrible rage inside Duncan, and he lunged at her, wrenching at the underwear. There was a silent struggle between them, free of games or deceit. Their feelings were too violent to be controlled. She flailed at him, releasing months of hurt and humiliation. He, overcome by shocked rage, tugged hysterically at the black underwear. Neither of them noticed the ripping silk, the overturned chairs, the mighty crash of shattering glass as they stumbled into the drinks tray. Still they fought on. Eventually, Flora wrenched away from him.

Duncan, suffused by anger and pain, shouted: 'Oh, yes, you'll always love me! My God, you call this carnage love?'

'It's the memory of you I'll love,' Flora said. 'I'll always love you as you were, when we first met.'

'What do you know of love?' Duncan said bitterly. 'You know nothing about it. Nothing. It was just sex with her, Flora. Sex.'

'How stupid of me,' she said. 'I tend to confuse the two.'

Duncan, reeling from the rancour in her voice, scooped up the whisky bottle. 'You didn't do this alone. No way did you do this alone.' She said nothing. Duncan suddenly saw the implacable face of Mark Hollister; the malevolent gleam behind those creepy glasses. 'Of course,' he said. 'Mark. Two queen bitches. My God, what an unholy alliance.'

'Is that all you can think of?' Flora said quietly. 'What

about our son? Tell me, how does he score on your scale of importance?' He looked at her uncomprehendingly. 'He doesn't want to live under the same roof as you, did you know that? He said he didn't even want to breathe the same air. Children have such candour, don't they?'

Duncan just stared at Flora, standing before him in the torn black underwear. He was looking at a stranger. He felt faint, the room was beginning to reel around him. 'That suits me just fine,' he said. 'The air around here has been stale for years.'

He picked up his clothes and moved unsteadily towards the door. At the doorway he paused and looked back, agonisingly aware of all that he had lost and all he was about to lose. 'Tell me,' he said, 'what you've done . . . has it made you feel ugly?'

'I've never considered myself to be anything else,' Flora said.

The bluntness of her reply touched a chord in him. 'In God's name, Flora. You said you forgave me?'

She looked up and met his eyes. 'I lied,' she said.

As Duncan turned and went out of the door, Flora slumped to her knees in front of the fire. The front door slammed and the tears broke. She heard Duncan's car driving away and she put her arms around herself and hugged herself, rocking backwards and forwards in front of the dying fire. She, too, was engulfed by loss.

Epilogue

The Returning Officer for the Carlingham constituency was reading out the by-election results. 'Martin David Donahue . . .'

'Labour,' murmured the political commentator in the studio.

'Six thousand, four hundred and eleven.'

Donnie looked around for the new director of *Face the Famous*. 'Allie, it's on now.'

Alison Sissons hurried in, drew up a chair at the desk next to Donnie and looked up anxiously at the television screen. 'Have I missed anything?'

'Labour six thousand something,' Donnie said. 'No. Ssh.'

'John Ambrose Loughton . . .'

'Liberal Democrat,' said the commentator, *sotto voce*.

'Fourteen thousand, two hundred and twenty-one.'

'There she is,' Allie said. 'Look. Right bang in the middle of the platform, big blue rosette. And those must be her children behind her. Don't they look happy, so sweet.'

'Flora Octavia Matlock . . .'

'Conservative . . .'

'Seventeen thousand, nine hundred and . . .'

There was a riotous burst of applause from the Carlingham crowd. The camera moved in on Flora as she smiled modestly, and then hugged Paul and Joanna and turned to thank each of her party workers.

'Brilliant,' Allie said. 'She made it.'

'What about that sharp suit, then?' Donnie said. 'And the new red hair.'

'Well, Duncan Matlock's estranged wife, standing in the by-election of his old constituency, has won the day,' the commentator said. 'A sympathy vote? Who can say?'

'She's certainly got some pretty heavyweight support,' Donnie said. 'Isn't that Sir Donald Frazier clapping madly over there on the right?'

'He looks so pleased and proud,' Allie said. 'As though he were her father.'

'Or her lover?' Donnie said.

'Don't be silly,' said Allie. 'He's far too old. Look there, behind Flora. The constituency battleaxe.'

'. . . Rosalind Clegg, the new chairman of the local Conservative Association, who was so integral to Mrs Matlock's candidature . . .' the commentator was saying. 'And I see Mark Hollister there, Duncan Matlock's old Ministerial adviser. Does his presence signify Flora Matlock's intention to follow in her husband's footsteps?' The crowd outside the Town Hall was still roaring its approval. 'All questions for the future. Right now, she's savouring the moment of her triumph. And I'm sure everyone sitting at home, watching this, will feel that it's a triumph she has certainly earned.'

'Hear, hear,' said Allie.

The camera zoomed in for a close-up of Flora, flushed and euphoric.

'I may be wrong,' Donnie said, 'but don't I detect just the tiniest tinge of the Iron Lady?'

Allie peered at the screen. Was there a certain set to Flora Matlock's jaw? A new toughness about her that wasn't evident those many months ago when she was just the politician's wife? 'No, Donnie,' she said. 'It's just a trick of the light.'

Flora was moving towards the microphone now, to make her acceptance speech. 'One can't help but speculate,' the commentator was saying, 'how Duncan Matlock, who is about to take up his post in Brussels as Parliamentary Adviser to an EEC think-tank on customs controls – one can't help but wonder how he feels about this extraordinary turn of events.'

'Mr Returning Officer, my Lord Mayor, ladies and gentlemen. First of all, I would like to thank my fellow candidates for the decency and dignity they have displayed throughout this campaign . . .'

Duncan was sitting at the bar in Heathrow Airport, gazing blankly at a television screen. His face showed no emotion as he watched his wife graciously accept his old job. Flora seemed as much a stranger to him up there on the television as she had seemed on that dreadful night in Mindermere, when she'd come into his study dressed up in Jennifer's black silk thing.

The airport tannoy crackled: 'We are pleased to announce that BA Flight 124 to Brussels is now ready for boarding . . .'

Brussels? Duncan drained his drink. Maybe, he thought to himself, the pro-Europeans had got it right, after all. Maybe the centre of power was shifting . . .

He picked up his bags and walked briskly through the departure gate.

TOM McGREGOR

The Knock

One of law-enforcement's best-kept secrets – a crack team of young investigators out to catch the customs and excise fraudsters. Working from top-security headquarters, often undercover, the Knock is enough to strike fear into the heart of the most hardened criminal.

Bill Adams is the paternal boss who rules his teams with a rod of iron. From tough South Londoner Gerry Birch, worried by financial problems, to Diane Ralston, hard-headed senior officer at the airport, all the team members rely on the camaraderie they share to get them through the tense, exhilarating, life-threatening situations they face.

But when the teams are undermined, by illness and by personal pressures, rifts start to develop which threaten to betray the whole operation . . .

Taut, authentic, gritty, set against a backdrop of drug-trafficking and international fraud, *The Knock* reveals the conflicts and triumphs of a dedicated team.

Based on the series created and written by Anita Bronson
A Bronson Knight Production for LWT

MARCELLE BERNSTEIN

Body and Soul

'She stretched her arms wider, back muscles aching, bloodless fingers numb, for the remaining minutes of the psalm. She wanted to hurt her faithless body, that had so easily forgotten that she was a woman set apart.'

When her brother's suicide forces Anna, an enclosed nun, into the world outside to try and save his yarn-spinning mill and help his family, she finds herself caught up in her own crisis of doubts and longings.

'Memorably erotic'
Daily Mail

'Read it and love it. A beautiful story'
New Woman

'A very passionate novel, very perceptive and very understanding'
Publishing News

LYNDA LA PLANTE

Prime Suspect III

Newly assigned to the vice squad, Soho Division, DCI Jane Tennison finds herself thrown in at the deep end of a particularly disturbing case.

The charred body of a murdered rent boy has been found. It marks the start of an horrific journey into the dark underbelly of society – where young runaway children are casually exploited for the gratification of perverted men.

And for Tennison it means that she will be up against it as never before. Battling against double-dealing and high-level corruption, she must cut to the rotten heart of the investigation – no matter who gets hurt on the way . . .

Prime Suspect III is a Granada Television Production starring Helen Mirren as DCI Tennison

Produced by Paul Markus
Executive Producer: Sally Head
Directed by David Drury

A List of Film and TV Tie-In Titles
Available from Mandarin

While every effort is made to keep prices low, it is sometimes necessary to increase prices at short notice. Mandarin Paperbacks reserves the right to show new retail prices on covers which may differ from those previously advertised in the text or elsewhere.

The prices shown below were correct at the time of going to press.